P9-DDM-984

Praise for
REVENGE OF THE RED CLUB

"With unauthorized leggings, tampons carried openly, and period-speak that—ahem, flows—in the hallways, this middle school #MeToo movement will educate and inspire budding feminists. . . . A real and necessary read, period!" —*Kirkus Reviews*

"This is a must-have for every upper elementary and middle school collection, where the topic of menstruation is not often centered in fictional narratives. . . . A middle school feminist manifesto that fans of girl-led ensembles like Ann M. Martin's the Baby-Sitters Club and Ann Brashares's *The Sisterhood of the Traveling Pants* will love, and that will inspire future Red Clubs in the process." —*SLJ*

NOV 2020

REVENGE of the Red CLUB

KIM HARRINGTON

ALADDIN

NEW YORK LONDON TORONTO SYDNEY NEW DELHI

Mount Laurel Library
100 Walt Whitman Avenue
Mount Laurel, NJ 08054-9539
856-234-7319
www.mountlaurellibrary.org

If you purchased this book without a cover, you should be aware that this book is stolen property. It was reported as "unsold and destroyed" to the publisher, and neither the author nor the publisher has received any payment for this "stripped book."

This book is a work of fiction. Any references to historical events, real people, or real places are used fictitiously. Other names, characters, places, and events are products of the author's imagination, and any resemblance to actual events or places or persons, living or dead, is entirely coincidental.

ALADDIN
An imprint of Simon & Schuster Children's Publishing Division
1230 Avenue of the Americas, New York, New York 10020
First Aladdin paperback edition October 2020
Text copyright © 2019 by Kim Harrington
Cover illustration and hand-lettering copyright © 2019 by Risa Rodil
Also available in an Aladdin hardcover edition.
All rights reserved, including the right of reproduction in whole or in part in any form.
ALADDIN and related logo are registered trademarks of Simon & Schuster, Inc.
For information about special discounts for bulk purchases, please contact
Simon & Schuster Special Sales at 1-866-506-1949 or business@simonandschuster.com.
The Simon & Schuster Speakers Bureau can bring authors to your live event. For more information or to book an event contact the Simon & Schuster Speakers Bureau at 1-866-248-3049 or visit our website at www.simonspeakers.com.
Book designed by Tiara Iandiorio
The text of this book was set in Chaparral Pro.
Manufactured in the United States of America 0920 OFF
2 4 6 8 10 9 7 5 3 1
The Library of Congress has cataloged the hardcover edition as follows:
Names: Harrington, Kim, 1974– author.
Title: Revenge of the Red Club / by Kim Harrington.
Description: First Aladdin hardcover edition. | New York : Aladdin, 2019. |
Summary: When middle school journalist Riley Dunne learns that an important and beloved club is being shut down, she uses the power of the pen to instigate much-needed social change.
Identifiers: LCCN 2018061279 (print) | LCCN 2019001450 (eBook) |
ISBN 9781534435742 (eBook) | ISBN 9781534435728 (hc)
Subjects: | CYAC: Reporters and reporting—Fiction. | Clubs—Fiction. | Social change—Fiction. | Middle schools—Fiction. | Schools—Fiction. | Family life—Massachusetts—Fiction. | Massachusetts—Fiction.
Classification: LCC PZ7.H23817 (eBook) | LCC PZ7.H23817 Rev 2019 (print) |
DDC [Fic]—dc23
LC record available at https://lccn.loc.gov/2018061279
ISBN 9781534435735 (pbk)

To Mom

CHAPTER 1

WE WEREN'T SUPPOSED TO LOOK AT OUR
phones during school hours, but I slid mine out of
my pocket anyway. I had to see if the new edition of
the *Hawking Observer* had posted. My middle school's
newspaper was hosted on the school website. We had a
sportswriter, an advice columnist, a reviewer, and one
intrepid investigative reporter (that was me).

I loved seeing my byline, Riley Dunne, beneath
a story. Though one of these days I had to get a new
photo. The one they used was from two years ago, when
I'd entered Hawking Middle in sixth grade. Sure, I still

had the same mousy-brown hair and wore the same hoodie-and-jeans ensemble most days. But now I was two years older and had recently gotten my braces off.

This new article was a biggie. I'd completed an in-depth investigation into the supposedly gluten-free chicken nuggets at lunch, which had given my friend Cee a no good, very bad day. She had celiac disease, so eating anything with gluten was harmful. After some before-school cabinet snooping, I'd found that our cafeteria's food supplier had switched brands, and the new breading was certainly not gluten-free.

I refreshed the page again. Still no update. I hoped my editor hadn't killed the story. But Ms. Bhatt was usually pretty cool about my investigative reports, and she hadn't mentioned having a problem with the article.

Math class was going to start any minute, so I put my phone away. Then I looked up and saw the new girl, Julia Alpert, coming down the aisle in white jeans and a cute purple top that stopped right at the waistband. She seemed sweet, but kind of shy.

Stella Duval looked her up and down from one row over. "You're not supposed to wear white pants after Labor Day. You know that, right?"

Stella had more rules for fashion than the entire

US government had laws. She dressed each day like school was a beauty pageant, which wouldn't be bad if she didn't judge other people who didn't go all out. Personally, I thought if you wanted to wear sweats, go for it. You wanted to wear a dress and heels when it was snowing out? Get it, girl. But Stella had somehow appointed herself the unelected fashion judge of our school.

Julia didn't respond. She just stared down at her desk. I opened my mouth to make a snarky comment back to Stella, but before I could, Mr. Barlow blew into the room like a human tornado. Papers flew off the top of the pile he was carrying, and he nearly knocked over a cup of coffee on his desk when he laid them down.

"I have your tests graded," he announced, and a rumble of nervous chatter went through the room. Chairs squeaked as kids shifted in their seats.

With that news at the forefront of my brain, I stopped thinking about my article and started worrying about algebra. It was a tough class in general, but that test had been even harder than most. Mr. Barlow walked the aisle, passing the exams back facedown on students' desks. This was supposed to somehow keep students' grades private. But you knew exactly how someone did as soon as they flipped their test over. Eighth graders weren't exactly known for their poker faces.

I watched as Ava, my best friend, got her test in the seat beside me. Her face fell, and I saw a flash of a seventy-something as she slapped the test back down. She hadn't studied much. She hadn't had time. Ava was a competitive gymnast. Her parents drove her forty minutes almost every day to an award-winning gym because she'd surpassed the one here in town. Even weekends, for hours and hours. Ava was good. Like Olympics good, in my opinion. But because of all the time she put into gymnastics, she didn't have as much time for other things—like grades, having a social life, etcetera. I was the only friend she actually spent time with outside of school. We'd lived next door to each other our whole lives, but it was getting harder to find time to get together.

Mr. Barlow headed down my row next. My stomach curled up into a tiny ball. I tried to look for any hint in his face, like disappointment, or *OMG, you totally rocked this*. But I saw nothing. This test was so hard. What if I'd bombed it?

He placed the paper facedown and moved on behind me. I gingerly turned it over. Eighty-nine! I blew out a breath so hard it almost blew my test off my desk.

"I know this test was difficult," he said, returning to the front of the classroom. "But I'm not here to hand out easy As. I'm here to challenge you. And I think every single one of you can rise to that challenge if you put the effort in."

He lifted a marker and wrote a problem on the whiteboard. "Everyone got number three wrong, so we're going to go over that one together. I need a volunteer for the board."

No one raised their hand.

"Okay, I'll just call on someone." His eyes scanned the room. I immediately began rummaging in my backpack on the floor. He certainly wouldn't call on me if I was super busy looking for a pencil or whatnot.

"Julia."

It worked!

Poor Julia, though. What a day. First Stella called her out on her post–Labor Day wear, and now this. But as she stood up to walk to the board, things suddenly got way, way worse.

Julia had an uninvited guest—Aunt Flo, the most obnoxious, unwelcome visitor. And Julia certainly hadn't been expecting Flo to show up. I didn't think she even knew she was here. But due to that dark red stain on her white jeans, the whole class would know soon.

Julia started her walk down the aisle.

I yanked my hoodie over my head. I'd be cold in just a T-shirt, but this was more important. I ripped a sheet of paper from my notebook and stuffed it in my pocket. Then I dashed down the aisle, swooped my arms around her, and quickly tied the sweatshirt around her waist.

"You need this," I whispered.

I continued down the aisle and tossed the crumpled-up piece of paper from my pocket into the trash. Then I casually walked back to my seat. *Nothing to see here. Just had to throw some scrap paper away.*

But unfortunately, some people had seen. Bad people. The front of the class was oblivious, but Brody Scruggs and a couple of his buddies from the back were snickering and laughing with one another.

Mr. Barlow turned around. "Is there a problem?"

They clammed up and shook their heads. But as soon as Mr. Barlow turned away to hand the marker to Julia, evil grins spread across their faces once again.

Ava gave me a nod and whispered, "Good work," under her breath.

I only wished I'd been faster. Or that Julia's Aunt Flo hadn't decided to visit on a day that she got called up to the board. Or that she hadn't broken the Labor Day white-pants rule.

"I hope you're not going to take that sweatshirt back," Brody sneered.

"Why wouldn't I?" I asked, giving him a fake bewildered look.

He rolled his eyes. "You know why."

I shrugged. "I really don't."

Mr. Barlow turned around. "Is there a problem in the back of the room?"

I nonchalantly began scribbling numbers in my notebook, not a care in the world. Brody huffed beside me. But I doubted that he was upset about getting in trouble for talking. He got in trouble a thousand times a day. What had really gotten under his skin was that he was unable to get under mine. I didn't give him the satisfaction of getting upset, and I wouldn't let Julia do it either.

I smiled as I looked at the numbers I'd written down. It was time to introduce the new girl to the Red Club.

CHAPTER 2

WHEN THE BELL RANG, JULIA TURNED IN
her seat. "Riley, thanks for the . . . um . . ."

I waved her off. "No worries. Give me my sweatshirt
back another day. But in the meantime, before you go
to lunch I have something to show you."

She raised one eyebrow, which was pretty cool. I
tried to do that in a mirror once, but I only looked like a
really confused person painfully raising both eyebrows.

"Just trust me," I said.

Ava sidled up next to us as we walked out of the
classroom. "Riley, heading to lunch, right?"

"Yeah, I just have to show Julia the thing."

"The thing?" Julia repeated, a little nervous now.

"You know." I widened my eyes at Ava. "The *thing*."

Ava let out a little groan. "Oh. The thing that I'm not in."

"Yet!" I reminded her. Then I guided Julia by the arm. "This way."

Ava went on her own to lunch, which she didn't seem happy about. But as a club member, I had a responsibility. Lunch had to wait.

Hawking Middle School was shaped like a giant square, with four connecting hallways and a big open courtyard in the middle that we never really used because it was cold most of the year in Massachusetts.

"I really need to stop by the bathroom," Julia whispered.

"I know. That's all part of this. Don't worry. We're almost there."

My eyes scanned the locker numbers as they counted down. We were in the thirties, then twenties, then teens.

"Here we are," I said, stopping at locker number one.

Julia looked from the locker to me as if I were crazy. "You brought me to your locker?"

"I brought you to *our* locker."

"'Our'?" Julia looked even more confused now.

"This is the locker of the Red Club, which you are now a part of." I handed her the sheet of paper I'd written the numbers on. This was always my favorite part. Like I was bestowing an honor on a fellow member.

But she didn't look impressed. "I don't get it."

And I forgot. She was new to our school. She didn't know.

"That's the combination." I motioned to the lock. "Open it."

Still skeptical and probably desperately wanting to hit the bathroom, Julia spun the numbers on the dial and pulled open the door.

Nothing amazing happened. No music played. No Red Club banner adorned the inside. It looked plain, actually, with a paper grocery bag on one shelf and a plastic bag on another.

"What is this?" she asked.

"This is our emergency stash," I said. "Once you're a Red Club member, you have the combination and you can use it if you are in need."

I reached for the bag on the top shelf. "Pads and tampons are in here." Then I showed her the bottom shelf. "Three pairs of sweatpants in there, various sizes. Just wash them and return them to the locker."

Her face brightened. "I can change into a pair of those right now?"

"Yep! And do you need a tampon, or do you have one in your bag?"

"Um, I don't . . ."

I scrunched up my forehead. "Is this your first time?"

"No, I had it once before, over the summer. But then it didn't come again for a few months."

I nodded quickly. "That happened to a friend of mine in the club. People expect to get it on the regular right after their first one, but it doesn't always work that way."

Julia stared at the bag of period paraphernalia, looking overwhelmed.

"Just take a couple of pads for now," I said. "We'll talk more at the meeting this afternoon."

"Meeting?" she repeated.

"The Red Club meets in the library after school every Wednesday. You don't have to come. But I think you'd really like it if you did."

"It's like a support group?" she asked.

"That and more."

The tightness in her shoulders seemed to release. "That sounds nice. I'll be there."

Julia bounded off to the bathroom, pads and sweatpants shoved in her backpack. I reached across my shoulder and gave myself a little pat on the back. Job well done. And now, time for lunch. My stomach growled angrily. But Ava would be even angrier. She hated it if I missed lunchtime with her for any reason. She was my best friend and I loved her, but sometimes she acted like she was my boss. I quickened my step, even though I was only a couple of minutes late.

The intercom clicked on and the principal's voice boomed through the hallway speakers. "Riley Dunne, please report to the office."

I swallowed hard. It looked like I was about to be *very* late.

CHAPTER 3

THIS WASN'T THE FIRST TIME I'D BEEN IN Principal Pickford's office. I wasn't a troublemaker, not in the traditional sense. But I didn't back down from the truth, and that sometimes landed me in this uncomfortable, stiff-backed chair staring at the framed photographs Pickford kept on his walls. Most of them looked like Florida, and one was my favorite—a single palm tree on a beach.

"Riley," he said, pulling my attention away from the beach and toward him. He wasn't mad. I knew his angry face. And there was a rumor that his shiny dome of a head glowed red when he got really upset, though I'd never seen that for myself. Today he just looked . . . tired. "You're a good student."

"Thank you, sir."

He clasped his hands on the top of his dark wood desk. "I don't like bringing you in here."

"I don't like being in here, sir." I added quickly, "No offense."

He considered me for a moment through his circular wire-rimmed glasses. "Do you know how busy I am?"

I assumed this was a rhetorical question, so I stayed silent.

He continued. "Very busy. This is a twenty-four-hours-a-day job. I get phone calls and e-mails around the clock. I am responsible for every teacher, staff member, and student in this building. Sometimes I lie awake at night thinking about the problems I'm going to have to face the next day. So, do you know who my favorite students are?"

Assuming this was another rhetorical question, I kept my mouth shut.

"The ones I never have to see," he answered. "The ones who don't make me get frustrated e-mails or angry phone calls. The ones who don't cause trouble for me—"

"Sir," I interrupted. "Why am I here?"

He jiggled the mouse on his mouse pad, and the screen saver on his monitor dissolved. Behind it was today's edition of the *Hawking Observer*, with my story at the top. It had posted!

"This story went up thirty minutes ago," Principal Pickford said. "And I've already gotten two phone calls. *Two*."

"From people thankful that the cafeteria is going to be more careful now?"

He let out a groan. "No. They were not . . . *thankful*."

I straightened my shoulders. "Well, they should be. Because of that investigative report, the cafeteria will be extra careful from now on when their supplier changes ingredients."

"Because of that article," he said, "people are going to panic and think that their children aren't safe here. This is all blown out of proportion. The cafeteria made a simple oversight—"

"An oversight that caused Cee to miss half a day of school," I cut in.

He sighed heavily. "If Cee felt that something was improperly labeled, she should have gone through the appropriate channels, not to an eighth-grade school-newspaper reporter."

I crossed my arms. "The bottom line is this. Cee had been eating those gluten-free nuggets for two years. But then they changed brands, didn't check carefully, and didn't remove the words 'gluten-free' from the menu. Now, because of my article, they'll check *everything* carefully when there's a change. And not just for gluten, but for allergens like peanuts. You wouldn't want a careless supplier to cause a child to go into anaphylactic shock, would you?"

He snorted. "Of course not."

I slid out my reporter's notebook from my bag like I was going to take a quote. "You're not telling me I should have covered up their mistake, are you?"

"No, I'm not saying that!"

"Then what are you saying, Mr. Pickford?"

He pinched the bridge of his nose. "You're dismissed, Riley."

I stood up quickly, shoving my notebook back into my bag. "Okay, Mr. Pickford. Thanks!" I tried not to let him see my giant smile of satisfaction on the way out.

By the time I got to my lunch table, Ava had nearly finished her salad. I pulled the sandwich out of my brown paper bag and took a huge bite.

"What was that about?" Ava asked as she reached

up to tighten her blond ponytail. She wore her hair in a ponytail all the time, even when she wasn't practicing. "I heard your name on the intercom."

I chewed for a moment. "My latest investigative report didn't go over too well."

Her eyes widened. "Are you in trouble?"

"I was at first, kind of, but not anymore." I tore off another bite and chewed it quickly.

"How did you get out of it?"

"I used words."

She nodded. "You're good with those."

My dad had this theory that everyone was born with something special. He called it a superskill—like a superpower, but instead of being able to fly, you could just cook really well or whatever. Ava was an amazing gymnast. My friend Cee had a head for business. My grandmother could take the most pathetic, half-dead plant and bring it back to life, every time. So far, my little brother's only gift seemed to be an unlimited supply of gas. But my dad said that sometimes it took years for someone to find their superskill. I was lucky: I found mine early on.

Words.

I used them to change people's minds, to change people's moods. They were just a selection of letters put together in different ways, but words were so powerful. They could change the world.

"So, long story short, I was thinking that I could fit you in today."

Unfortunately, I hadn't been listening to Ava's words. "Um, today?"

She nodded with a big smile. "Yeah, right after school for like an hour. We could hang out at my house. I could show you the video of my competition last week."

Ahhh, she wanted to hang out. "I can't today. I have a club after school."

"I have ice cream," she offered, knowing my love for ice cream had no bounds.

But I had to say no. Not even my beloved ice cream could pull me away from the Red Club. "I really can't. I have a meeting."

Ava's smile fell. "So skip it. This is the only hour that I have free this week."

I stared down at my sandwich, the jelly oozing over the side of the crust. I felt bad that Ava was so busy all the time. And I was the only one she really hung out with outside school. But I couldn't just drop my plans when she finally had an hour free.

"I can't," I said. "This is an important meeting."

She rolled her eyes. "Fine. I'll just go with you, then. At least we'll be hanging out together. What is the meeting for? The newspaper?"

I chewed on my lower lip. "Um, no. You know what I have on Wednesdays."

Ava's face reddened. "Oh. The club I'll never get to join."

"That's not true," I protested.

Ava had been frustrated lately that she hadn't gotten her period yet. She claimed that she was the "last eighth grader on earth" without it, but obviously that wasn't true.

I reached across the table and grabbed her hand. "Remember what your mom said. *Everyone has their own timetable.* And because you're so active, and your mom got hers later, you'll probably get yours later too."

Her eyes glistened. "I just feel like such a weirdo. Everyone else is going through this thing together, and I'm the outsider. You've had yours for years!"

"I haven't had it *that* long," I said. "And believe me, it's not that great. Once you get it, you'll wish you hadn't been in such a hurry. We're talking cramps, zits, bloating, mood swings. Sometimes I look in the toilet and it's like I sacrificed a goat."

She burst out laughing. "Stop! Oh my gosh, stop."

"Feel better?" I asked.

She nodded. "Except now my cheeks hurt from laughing."

I felt a swell of pride. I'd taken a friend from hurting to laughing. I'd done that with my own words. And after school the Red Club would make Julia feel better too.

CHAPTER 4

AS SOON AS THE LAST BELL RANG, I hopped up from my seat and hurried to the school library. My friend Cee Butler was already there, her feet propped up on a desk. Her hair fell in long black braids, with one of the front ones wrapped in purple. A book about business marketing covered most of her face.

Even though the Red Club never technically had presidents, Cee ran the meetings this year. Cee's real name was Cynthia, but we'd started calling her CEO a couple of years ago when she started her own business.

Along the way that got shortened to Cee-O and then eventually just Cee. She didn't mind the nickname. She said it was quicker to say than Cynthia and therefore more efficient.

I dropped my backpack on the floor and took the seat beside her. "I've been meaning to ask you—how'd you do at that garage sale?" Cee bought old jewelry at garage sales and cleaned it up. Then she took pictures of the pieces on cute models with flattering filters and resold it for much more online.

"Pretty well," Cee said from behind the book. "I got a brooch for a dollar and resold it the same day for twenty. It's amazing what people will pay if you use the word 'vintage' instead of 'old.'"

Cee had an eye for business and fashion. I would never know if a random piece of jewelry on a yard-sale table was worthless trash or treasure. But she had an instinct for it. She'd take a dowdy-looking necklace, pair it with just the right blouse to bring out its "potential" in the photo, and boom—sale.

She lowered the book just enough for me to see her big brown eyes. "I heard you had a busy day. Saved the new girl from embarrassment and got in trouble for the article."

I shrugged. "Mild trouble. I'm not worried about

it. It's more important that you can trust the food you're given."

"Thanks, Riley. I can always count on you." Smiling, she shoved the book into her bag and brought her feet down from the desk.

Stella strolled in with Camille Flores beside her, whispering in each other's ears. They were best friends, though they argued as much as they got along. They were opposites in many ways, but the Red Club had brought them together. The Red Club was always building bonds and forming friendships.

Stella, fashion queen, had fiery red hair against her pale face. Camille's long black hair hung to her waist and swished back and forth when she walked. She had tan skin and the perfect bone structure of her mother, who'd been a model in Brazil before she came to the United States. But Camille wanted no part of the modeling world. She wanted to be a stand-up comedian, which raised eyebrows when she told people—especially grown-ups. But she was legitimately funny, and I thought she could totally do it.

A bunch of other girls arrived, but still no Julia.

"Is the new girl coming?" Stella asked, holding her hand out to examine her manicure. "If anyone needs some Red Club today, it's her."

"You didn't exactly help make her day shine with your comment about her clothes," I pointed out.

Stella looked up at me. "Well, I was right, wasn't I? If she had followed the rule, she wouldn't have had to deal with Brody taunting her all day and calling her 'Bloody Julia.'"

Ugh. He did? All day? I gritted my teeth.

As if we had conjured him by saying his name, Brody and one of his friends loudly stopped near the open double doors to the library. His friend, in full soccer gear, was holding a towel to his profusely bleeding face.

Brody ran a hand over his spiky black hair and said, "Cool, man. You really ate it out there. Let me see."

The boy tentatively lifted the towel.

Brody reared back. "Wow! Bloody nose *and* a missing tooth! Oh man."

They continued toward the nurse's office while Brody's laughter carried down the hall.

My hands curled into fists. "Does anyone else see the irony in that?"

Cee snorted. "Blood from a boy's nose and mouth in a horrific injury is 'cool.' But blood from a girl in a natural monthly process is disgusting."

"And shameful," I added. "He shamed her all day. For something normal and natural."

A giggling group of seventh graders piled in and sat in the back. Julia snuck in behind them, head down, eyes shifting around nervously. I knew she wouldn't want to be the center of attention, so I didn't mention anything about her induction.

"Call to order," I whispered to Cee.

Nodding, Cee stood and clapped her hands. "Good afternoon, Red Club members. Who wants the floor?"

A normally quiet sixth grader named Kristy who'd been inducted last month raised her hand. "My cramps are so bad. I feel like there's an angry little man in my stomach, just repeatedly punching my uterus."

"My angry little man squeezes," another girl said. "Like my insides are his stress ball."

"Have you tried a heating pad or a hot-water bottle?" Stella asked. "It really helps."

"Sure, when you're at home," Kristy said. "But I can't whip out a heating pad in the middle of English class."

"Or can you?" Camille stood and pulled something out of her backpack. "I just put a couple of these in the special locker. My mom bought them for me, and they worked so well I knew we had to have a stash for the club."

She passed them forward, and I took a look. It was like a big sticker. "You just pull the back off and stick it on?" I asked.

"Yeah," Camille said. "It heats up and stays warm for a long time. You can't see it under your clothes, either."

I handed it to Kristy, whose face had lit up. "Cool, thanks! This is going to help."

A warm feeling spread through my chest. That was exactly what this club was for—helping one another. I loved it so much. And I always learned something new at every meeting. Until a minute ago, I hadn't even known stick-on heating pads existed.

"Anyone else?" Cee asked.

From the back, a tiny hand popped up into the air. Julia's hand.

"Julia," Cee said, pointing. "We're all here if you need to vent about today."

"Um, no," she said, blushing. "I just have a question."

"Go for it," Cee said. "You can say anything here."

Julia's face turned even redder. "Um, my mom says you have to be older to use a tampon. Do any of you use tampons?"

Stella piped up. "Of course! Listen, you totally want to use tampons. Pads feel like diapers."

"But pads are easy," Camille said. "I'm scared of tampons."

Stella rolled her eyes. "They're not scary. You can't even feel it if it's in right. And you can go swimming."

"It's October!" Camille said. "No one is going swimming."

"Guys, guys," Cee cut in. "I appreciate your Team Pad and Team Tampon enthusiasm, but there is no one right choice. And it's for Julia to decide, not us."

"Anyone else poop more when they have their period?" a seventh grader, Paige, blurted. Her friends giggled beside her. "I feel like I have the pooponic plague."

A few other girls laughed nervously. But I'd sat in so many of these meetings over the last two years that I'd heard it all. I'd spent the first year listening and learning, and now I could give back.

Stella gagged. "TMI, Paige. C'mon, gross."

I raised a finger in the air. "No, not gross! That's the point of this club. It's where we can ask questions and talk about this kind of stuff and *not* be judged. Not be called gross."

"Riley's right," Cee said. "It's all natural. And yes, I poop a little more during Shark Week."

Stella rolled her eyes as if this was all a bit too

uncouth for her. But at the same time, she had the hint of a smile at the corner of her mouth. After all, if she didn't like the club, she wouldn't keep coming back. Membership wasn't forced on anyone. Most girls just came to meetings now and then, when they needed some support. Stella was here every week.

"Anyone else?" Cee asked.

"Can I ask a non-period question?" said a small voice from the back. It was a girl from my grade named Hazel. I didn't know her well. This was only her second meeting. She was quiet and artsy. I didn't know who she hung out with.

"Of course!" Cee said enthusiastically. "We're here for support, for anything."

Hazel took a deep breath. "Last night, my parents told me that they're separating. They're setting me up with, like, an adult professional to talk to, but I would also like to talk to someone my own age who has been through this."

"I have," Julia said. "That's part of why I moved here."

"Could we . . . ?" Hazel's voice trailed off.

"Do you have first or second lunch?" Julia asked.

"First," Hazel said. "Though I usually just eat in the library."

"Eat with me. I'd love to talk to someone who understands."

Hazel gave a huge smile, and Julia matched it.

I felt a burst of pride. This was why the Red Club was so powerful. It wasn't just about periods. It was about supporting one another.

"Anyone else?" Cee asked.

Stella raised her hand. "I'd just like to remind everyone that the dance committee is still looking for volunteers to decorate the gym. Anyone interested?"

Stella often used Red Club meetings as recruitment opportunities for her numerous other clubs. When no one raised their hand, she raised her voice. "The dance is next week, people! The theme is Falling into Autumn, and—"

Camille snorted. "What out-of-touch teacher came up with that dumb theme?"

Stella narrowed her eyes so hard, I thought flaming arrows would dart out of them. "*I* came up with the theme. And it's going to be beautiful." She stomped her foot on the floor for emphasis.

"Anything else?" Cee asked. After a few beats of silence, she picked up a book and lightly banged it on the table like a gavel. "Then this meeting of the Red Club is adjourned. Till next week!"

Everyone grabbed their backpacks and piled out the door.

"See you tomorrow!" Cee called to me over her shoulder.

"Bye!" I hiked my backpack up on one shoulder.

Julia approached me in the hall. "Hey, Riley. I just wanted to thank you for inviting me into the group. When that happened earlier today . . ." Her voice trailed off, and she shook her head.

"Try not to worry about it. Brody will be busy making someone else's life hell soon enough."

She smirked. "It helps knowing I have you guys. My mom isn't always willing to talk about this stuff."

"Same here," I said with a sigh.

"I wish they had a club like this at every school. I had so many friends at my old school who could have really used a Red Club. I hope you guys know how lucky you are."

I bumped her with my hip. "Well, you're one of us now, so you're lucky too."

She smiled. "How did the Red Club get started anyway?"

"None of us know. It seems to have been around forever." I explained, "I got my period early in sixth grade. I had a friend from the newspaper, Tonya, who was in eighth. She was the Cee of Red Club back then. So she told me about it."

"How did the other girls find out?" Julia asked.

I tapped my chin. "Let's see. Stella went to the nurse to get something for cramps, and later that day there was a note in her locker. Stella told some of her friends. I told Cee. Lots of girls already knew about it from older sisters."

"And then it just spreads?" she asked.

I nodded. "By the end of sixth grade, all the girls knew about the club—whether they could join yet or not. It probably happens like that every year."

"Like a passed-down tradition," she said.

"Totally. A tradition you're now a part of!"

Her smile took over her entire face but then quickly fell. "Oh no."

I glanced over my shoulder and saw Brody strutting toward us, back from escorting his friend to the nurse's office.

"Well, well," he yelled from down the hall. "Did I miss the *Bled* Club meeting?"

"Keep it moving, Brody," I snapped. "I'm sure there's a vulnerable sixth grader somewhere who you haven't picked on yet."

"But what if I'd rather pick on Bloody Julia?" he said with a sneer as he walked past.

I should have flung one of my snappy comebacks. Or, even better, ignored him. But as Julia's face contorted to hold back tears, something else happened instead. My foot took on a life of its own, separate from my rational brain, and edged itself into Brody's path. He tripped, his arms flailing out as a strangled cry escaped from his mouth. He landed on the floor with a hard slap as his hands broke his fall. And then, because now even my mouth was betraying my brain's signals . . . I laughed.

Brody scrambled up quickly, unhurt. But at my uncontrolled laughter, his face turned bright red. He pointed a finger at me and promised, "You'll pay for that."

As he staggered away, I looked down at my traitor of a foot. That wasn't me. I fought with words, not body parts! And then I glanced at Julia. Just a minute ago she'd been full of happiness and gratitude. Now she looked scared.

CHAPTER 5

I SET FOUR PLATES DOWN ON THE DINING room table as something in the living room caught my eye. Our house had an open floor plan. You could stand in the kitchen and basically see everything on the first floor. And right now my little brother, Danny, was sneaking up toward my dad, who was sitting innocently in his recliner reading a book. Danny grinned at me, and I knew exactly what was coming next. As he reached my father, he aimed his butt at his face and let one rip.

"Ugh!" Dad waved his hand in front of his face.

"Don't start a war you can't win, son. I had broccoli with lunch. Revenge will be served warm and smelly."

My mom looked up from her laptop on the couch and shook her head. "There's no decency in this house. What if we'd had guests over?"

Dad, still waving his hand, said, "We wouldn't have a fart war if we had people over."

"You shouldn't have a"—she paused, skipping over the word she couldn't even bear to say—"war like that at all. You go into the bathroom and do that in private. Nobody needs to hear about it."

As much as I thought my father and brother's fart wars were disgusting, I was on Team Dad here. He shared an office with his assistant. He had to hold those things in all day. At night, in the comfort of his own home, he should be able to let loose.

I loved my mom, but she was a delicate flower. In English class, we'd had to read this book from the 1800s, and there was a character who fainted all the time on her fainting couch, from the slightest thing. And I thought, *Hello, Mom. Fancy meeting you here in this old British novel.*

That was the main reason why I was so thankful for the Red Club. Mom never sat with me and had any kind of talk—about periods or whatever. She'd signed the permission slip for me to get the talk at school and figured that was enough. And sure, the school did an okay job of telling us what to expect. But questions pop up later, when you're in the middle of things. And I never felt comfortable asking my mom those questions, because she'd made it clear she didn't like "talk about things that should be private."

When Cee got her period, her mom celebrated her "womanhood" and baked her a cake. A cake! When I told my mom that I had received my first visit from Cousin Red, she nodded grimly and said, "The lower cabinet in the bathroom has supplies." That was it. No words of wisdom. Certainly no celebration of womanhood. It was treated like a shameful secret.

The Red Club let us talk about anything. We supported one another. We were more than just a locker with emergency pads. We were a sympathetic ear, a hug, a high five. We were whatever a member needed that day.

A timer in the kitchen dinged, and Dad jumped up from his seat. "My delicious masterpiece is ready!"

My family loved routine. Every night, Mom and Dad alternated who cooked. Then we'd play our game while we ate at the table. Danny and I took turns doing the dishes. Then we all sat in the living room together, even though we did separate things. I usually did my homework. Dad sat in his favorite chair and read one of his mystery novels. Danny played games on the iPad. And Mom watched house shows: buying houses, remodeling houses, decorating houses—she watched them all. She claimed that it helped in her job as a real estate agent, but I thought she'd still watch them no matter what her career was. She was a home-show addict.

Tonight had been my dad's turn to cook. He placed a steaming pasta casserole in the center of the table and yelled, "Come and get it!"

We all settled in and served ourselves; then Mom cleared her throat and asked, "Who wants to go first?"

The Dunne Family Dinner Game was cheesier than my dad's casserole, but my parents loved it. Every night, each one of us had to talk about one good thing that had happened that day and one thing we were looking forward to. On bad days, it could be a struggle. But what was weird was that searching my mind for those positive things ended up actually putting me in a better mood. Like magic or something.

"I'll go first, since no one else is volunteering," Dad said, making fake angry eyes at Danny and me. "I cracked a joke in a meeting today that made the big boss laugh. And what I'm looking forward to is watching Danny's soccer game this weekend."

"What was the joke?" Danny asked.

Dad's eyes got a little wider. "Um, I can't tell you that."

"But Daaaad," Danny whined.

"I'll go next," Mom said quickly. "I showed that house on Maple Road to a nice young family today, and I'm pretty sure they're going to put in an offer."

"That's great!" I said. I'd been listening to details about that house for weeks—from the updated kitchen to the new floors.

Mom added, "And I'm looking forward to a couple of things. First, my mother is coming to visit this weekend."

Danny and I shared a look. Anytime Grandma came to visit, she and Mom always ended up arguing.

"And the second thing I'm looking forward to," Mom continued, "is attending the school committee meeting tonight."

I nearly choked on my milk. "The thing you're looking forward to is sitting in a room and listening to a boring committee talk? Mom, I'm worried about you. Do you want to go to the movies tonight? Dad, I think you need to plan a date."

Dad and Danny both snorted.

Mom smiled but pointed a finger at me. "Community involvement is important. You know I always say that people who don't vote can't complain. It's the same here. We have no right to grumble about rules the committee makes if we're not involving ourselves when they're being made."

I nodded. "True. But I still think it's boring."

"Sometimes it is," she admitted. "But tonight should be interesting. The uptight-mom brigade is in full force lately, and Principal Pickford is getting sick of their calls and e-mails."

"Wait . . . *you're* calling another mom uptight?" I said with a grin.

Her face fell a bit. "Yep. There are worse moms than me. Who knew?"

My heart sank. I hadn't meant it like that. I was only kidding around. I didn't think she was a bad mom. Far from it. I hoped my joke hadn't hurt her feelings, but before I could open my mouth to explain, Danny started in on his turn. He couldn't decide what his favorite part of the day was, so he regaled us with five separate, long stories. From a nail-biter of a recess kickball game to his successfully blaming a fart on his class nemesis, we heard it all. And I was thankful once again that when he came to Hawking Middle next year, I would have moved on to high school.

Danny finally finished, and it was my turn, but I was undecided. The good part of my day had been helping Julia, but my mom had made it clear that she didn't approve of the Red Club. But to say that something else had been my good of the day would be a lie.

"I saved a girl," I blurted.

Dad paused with his fork in midair. "From what? Choking?"

"Um, no." I stared down at my almost empty plate. "She'd had her"—I gazed at my little brother—"monthly visitor during class and didn't realize it. The teacher called her up to the board. I knew it was going to be a disaster if everyone saw. So I wrapped my sweatshirt around her waist."

Danny snickered. "I know what that means. She got her *period*. Gross!"

Mom gasped. "Danny, please. I'm glad you're learning in health class, but women's trouble is not an appropriate topic for the dinner table."

I'd always hated that term. "Women's trouble." Like we'd done something wrong. And I didn't care if it was inappropriate for dinnertime. That was the good thing I'd done that day, and I was proud of it. Before I could stop myself, I added, "And the thing I'm looking forward to is next week's meeting of the Red Club, because today's meeting was great."

Mom's mouth turned down. "You're still in that . . . *club*? I figured you wouldn't need that anymore."

Part of me wished I'd never told her about the club to begin with, two years ago. Or that I hadn't brought it up again tonight. But it was important to me. I straightened my shoulders.

"Yes, I am still in the club. To help other girls. And for friendship. For sisterhood." Jeez, I sounded like a sorority chant. "It's not just about periods and stuff."

Mom pushed her plate away even though she hadn't yet finished.

"It's about girl power," I continued. "It's about supporting each other when we need it. Especially for the girls who—" I stopped myself before I could finish that sentence with *don't get support at home*.

Mom cleared her throat. "Well, I hope you don't share too much private information. It's not ladylike to talk about certain—"

"It *is* ladylike," I interrupted. "Because these things happen to *ladies*. It's natural. It's normal. It's nothing to be embarrassed of. I will never be ashamed of being a girl." My voice rose, and I gazed down at my hand and realized I'd clenched it into a fist.

"Okay, settle down," Dad chided. "No one's telling you to be ashamed."

Of course he didn't get it. Dad didn't know what it felt like to have to hide a tampon in your hand as you walked to the bathroom. But you couldn't take your backpack with you because then the whole class would know your dirty secret. How if you shook out an Advil from your purse in mixed company, you'd claim a headache before you admitted you had cramps. How if you got mad at a boy, he'd ask if it was "that time of the month" because you couldn't possibly have a legitimate reason to be angry. Dad didn't get it.

But Mom should have.

"May I be excused?" I asked.

Mom and Dad shared a look, like they were thinking about saying no.

"I'm finished eating. We finished our game. It's Danny's turn to do the dishes. And I'd like to get a start on my homework."

"That's fine," Dad said.

I quietly left the table, scooped my books up from the living room rug, and carried them to my room. I felt like being alone tonight.

CHAPTER 6

I STOOD IN HOMEROOM WHILE PRINCIPAL
Pickford's voice boomed over the intercom, leading the
school in the Pledge of Allegiance. Then we sat and
listened as the Leader of the Day read the morning
announcements. Today's lucky winner was a seventh
grader whose voice cracked three times. When we were
in elementary school, being Leader of the Day had been
awesome. When it was your turn, you'd felt special and
cool. Now it was just a chore.

The kid finished, and the intercom clicked off.

Ms. Bhatt, my homeroom teacher, turned to our

class and announced, "Julia, tomorrow you're going to be Leader of the Day!"

"I think you mean Bleeder of the Day," Brody muttered, and his dumb cronies snickered along.

I was hoping that Julia hadn't heard him, but by the sag in her shoulders I knew she had. She slumped down a bit in her chair, probably wishing she had an invisibility cloak. Though that definitely would have been more helpful the day before.

"Also," Ms. Bhatt said, "there's a short statement here that the principal would like all homeroom teachers to read out loud."

Ms. Bhatt was one of my favorite teachers. I had her for homeroom and science, and she was the newspaper advisor. She had long black hair that had a pretty wave to it. But her normally warm and friendly smile seemed stiff and fake this morning. Something was going on.

She cleared her throat and held the paper up as she read from it. "'The school committee last night, in partnership with Principal Pickford, vowed to take more seriously some rules that we've unfortunately let slide. We encourage all students to read the handbook and remind themselves of school policies.'"

Then she put the paper down and turned away.

That was it? That wasn't anything earth-shattering. It was just some vague blah blah blah. I'd read the handbook at the beginning of sixth grade, but it was pretty boring, and I'd never felt the need to read it again. I was sure everything was fine. The uptight-mom brigade had probably made everyone read the statement. Who knows why? Some people just like to be upset all the time.

There were only a couple of minutes left in homeroom, so most kids were packing up their stuff into their backpacks. I didn't need to, though. I had science first period, so I got to stay in Ms. Bhatt's room.

The bell rang, and Julia stopped at my desk, her backpack flung over one shoulder. "I'm sorry, Riley. I can't be in the Red Club."

"What? Why?" I asked, bewildered.

She let out a heavy sigh. "My mom won't let me. I asked her to buy tampons because I told her the other girls in the club said they're fine. But she said I'm not old enough and got upset. She said she doesn't think a club like that should be in school. I'm sorry."

"I hope she changes her mind," I said. Because what else could I say?

"Me too. I really enjoyed it."

I felt bad for Julia. It was a new school and a new

time in her life. She needed the support that the Red Club offered. But her mom seemed to have her mind made up, for now anyway.

Ms. Bhatt regained some of her usual cheer during science, but she still seemed a little bit off now and then. Like when she looked at me. Which was weird.

When the bell rang at the end of class, I made a special effort to stop by her desk on the way out. "Thanks, Ms. Bhatt! That was a really interesting lesson." It actually hadn't been, but I figured that might make her smile.

And it did, but her smile looked small and sad. "Thank you, Riley."

"I'll see you after school at the newspaper meeting!" I called over my shoulder.

And at that point her smile completely disappeared.

The rest of the morning passed uneventfully, and Brody even kept his mouth shut in math class. Maybe he'd finally gotten bored with bullying Julia. When it was time for lunch, I bought a slice of pizza and took my seat across from Ava. She wore her usual outfit— long T-shirt, black leggings, hair up in a ponytail.

"Did you hear about Sarah?" she asked, picking at her chicken sandwich.

I blotted some of the grease off my pizza slice with a napkin. "No, what's up?"

She leaned closer across the table and whispered, "She got dress-coded."

Sarah was in my science class. I tried to think back to what she'd been wearing, but nothing stuck out. No one ever got dress-coded, except one time when Becca wore a see-through mesh shirt, but that was obviously against the rules. Sarah wasn't wearing anything like that. I would have noticed.

"Why?" I asked.

Ava chewed through a bite. "Her tank-top strap was three finger widths apart, and it has to be at least four."

The real question was why Sarah would wear a tank top in October, but I'd leave that to Stella to judge. "Since when did they go measuring straps like that?"

Ava shrugged. "Must be a new rule."

I wondered if that was what that statement in homeroom had been about. They seemed to be enforcing rules that they'd never cared much about before. But then why didn't they just say that? *Hey, we've totally ignored the archaic dress code in our handbook for years, but we're going to start paying attention now.* I felt like there was more to it.

"Hey, there's some sort of commotion at that table." Ava motioned with her chin.

I glanced over my shoulder. Principal Pickford's assistant, a nice old lady we all called Miss Nancy, walked around, grim-faced, and pointed at certain girls. Whatever the selection meant, it wasn't good, because the girls all looked upset. They rose from their tables and left the cafeteria.

"What in the world is going on?" I asked.

"I don't know," Ava said, "but she's heading this way."

My heart sped up, even though I knew there was nothing to be afraid of. Miss Nancy was nice. Everyone loved her. She had a secret stash of candy she kept under her desk that she'd dole out if it seemed like you were having a bad day. But she didn't look like she was enjoying her job right now.

She approached our table and tilted her head, like she was looking for something underneath. I stared down. Was she checking out our shoes?

She lifted her arm and pointed at us. My stomach squeezed. *What? What did I do?*

"Ava," she called, "and Vanita."

Ava looked stunned across the table. Vanita, another eighth grader who was sitting next to us with her friends, asked, "What's going on?"

"You're both dress-coded," Miss Nancy said. "For leggings. Please head to the office."

Ava gasped.

My mouth dropped open.

Since when were leggings against the rules? Lots of girls wore leggings! Ava practically lived in them. She'd have to shop for an entire new wardrobe if this was really happening.

Vanita looked nervous, chewing on her bottom lip as she walked toward the door. Ava, however, looked mad.

On her way past my seat, she muttered two words under her breath: "Avenge me."

I nodded sternly and knew exactly what to do. My next investigative report would be about the grave injustice my best friend had faced at the hands of inconsistent dress-coding. The newspaper club was meeting right after school.

I couldn't wait to get started.

CHAPTER 7

I RUSHED TO MS. BHATT'S ROOM AT THE end of the day for the newspaper meeting. Cole Wallace, our sports reporter, was already sitting at a desk, but no one else. I stopped in the doorway, frozen.

Cole was in eighth grade like me. He was tall and skinny and walked a little hunched over, like he was worried that he would hit his head on a door frame. He was nice and polite and held the door for people, which was a small thing but something I noticed. But what I liked best about him was his smile. When he smiled, it made my stomach feel all fluttery. But not in a bad way.

"Um, are you going to walk into the room or not?" Lin asked with a laugh as she bumped into my back. Lin Cheung was only in sixth grade, but she always had the best suggestions in her advice column. And she saw right through me.

"Yeah, totally," I said, pretending to fix my backpack's position on my shoulder. "I was just on my way in."

She smirked. "Oh, so you weren't frozen in the doorway, too scared to be alone in a room with Cole where you'd have to make conversation?"

My mouth dropped open. *Seriously?* Was she psychic?

"Go," she whispered, nudging me. "He's just a *boy*."

Yeah, a boy who made my heart do cartwheels. A boy I maybe liked more than I liked ice cream. A boy who made me forget how to use words. Words! My superskill!

I took a deep breath and strolled in, doing my best imitation of normal human behavior. "Hey, Cole."

He looked up from the notebook he'd been writing in. "Oh hey, Riley! Hey, Lin!" He flashed that smile of his, and I sank down into the nearest chair before my legs turned to jelly.

"Just us three, huh?" he said. "Ms. Bhatt is never late. This is weird."

"And where's Niles?" I asked. Niles was the paper's reviewer, and he rounded out our small foursome.

Cole winced. "You didn't hear? He went to that new burger place last night to write a review, but he got food poisoning."

"Yuck." Lin grimaced. "Well, he'll have a lot to write about when he's done barfing."

"True," Cole said. "Hopefully he feels better in time for the dance next week. He'd mentioned that he was looking forward to it." Cole paused and glanced at me before quickly looking away. "Um, Riley, are you going?"

"Going where?" I asked, because all my brain cells suddenly went on strike.

"To the dance," he said, running a hand through his messy brown hair.

"Oh, I don't think so," I blurted. "I haven't really thought about it."

Lin gave me an angry face from her seat. *What?* I mouthed back. She shook her head.

And just when I thought I couldn't handle the awkwardness anymore, Ms. Bhatt finally came into the room. Normally, she was full of energy and positivity, wanting to hear our ideas. Today she stood before us with her hands clasped.

"I have some news," she said simply.

By her tone and the way that she didn't include the word "good," I assumed this was bad.

"What's going on?" Lin asked.

Ms. Bhatt looked at each of us. "The newspaper has a new advisor."

"But we don't want a new advisor," Cole said, and I agreed.

"The decision is out of my hands, unfortunately," she said.

What did that mean? What was happening? We all loved Ms. Bhatt. What if the new advisor was super picky? What if they censored us all the time? My heart started to pound heavily. I put a hand on my chest and tried to calm myself down. Maybe it wouldn't be so bad. Maybe the new person would be cool too.

With a little tremor in my voice, I asked, "So who's our new advisor?"

"Um, well—"

But before Ms. Bhatt could finish the sentence, the door swung open and Principal Pickford busted in. Ugh. Great timing. We were just about to find out something really important, and he was probably here to make sure no one was wearing short shorts.

He grinned widely. "Did you tell them the good news?"

Ms. Bhatt's eyes darted around the room. "I was just getting to it."

He stood in front of her and turned to face us. "Your new advisor . . . is me."

My stomach dropped. Cole's shoulders stiffened in the seat in front of me.

But Lin let out a giggle. "No, really," she said. "Who is it?"

Mr. Pickford frowned. "It's me. I'm your advisor."

"But . . . why?" Lin asked. "Ms. Bhatt was doing a great job."

He waved his hand at Lin dismissively. "Didn't you hear the announcement this morning? In partnership with the school committee, we've decided to buckle down on those darn handbook rules, and one of the rules is about club advisors. Ms. Bhatt doesn't have a lot of time for the newspaper. She's already the advisor for the science club and the nature club. The *Hawking Observer* deserves someone who can give it more attention. A closer eye."

I pinched my forearm in the hopes that this was a nightmare I could wake up from.

He clapped his hands together. "So, let's start our first meeting. What've we got? Tell me your ideas."

My mouth clamped shut like it had been stuck

with glue. I wasn't about to relay my excitement about a dramatic report on the unfairness of the old/new dress code.

Thankfully, Cole spoke up first. "In addition to my regular roundup of the results of our sports games for the week, I've been thinking about starting a new regular column. I'd interview one school athlete every week. We could talk about various things—how they prepare for games, working out and nutrition, scoping the competition."

"Wonderful idea!" Mr. Pickford boomed. "I think that's great. You're sprouting your wings and learning to fly."

Um, what?

Lin piped up next. "I had many letters come in this week looking for advice. It's always hard to choose, but I think I have it narrowed down to two."

"That's great. I'll want to read those first, of course," he said. "And Riley?"

I tried to swallow, but there appeared to be a giant lump of sand in my throat. "Nothing right now," I forced out.

"Okay, well, this was a great meeting. Just FYI, we're going to miss the next few editions as I create a framework of set guidelines for us to follow. But after that, we'll move forward with *responsible* journalism. I'm looking forward to it! I'll let you know, personally, when the next meeting will be."

Then he left.

The room seemed to tilt and sway. Echoes of his words bounced through my head.

Missing a few weeks.

Set guidelines.

Responsible journalism.

He'd become the new advisor so he could take control. He wanted to prevent us from provoking dialogue. He'd never let me run a story like the one on the dress code.

I sat stiffly in my chair until Lin came over and poked me with her pencil.

"Are you all right?"

I nodded. But I really wasn't.

"It'll be okay," she said.

I nodded. But it really wouldn't.

"He'll get bored with us. Or he'll get pulled into principal drama. And then we'll get Ms. Bhatt back again. Give it time. Everything will be fine."

I wasn't completely convinced, but I could breathe

again, so that was a start. I blinked and gazed around the room. Lin was the only one left. I hadn't even noticed Ms. Bhatt and Cole leave.

"Do you feel better?" she asked.

"A little."

"Good," she said, and then she punched my arm.

"Ow!" I cried. "What was that for?"

"For being an idiot! You've had a crush on Cole forever."

"So?"

"So, he asked you to the dance."

"What? No he didn't."

She raised her fist to punch my arm again, but I recoiled back. "Enough with the hitting!"

She put her hands on her hips. "He asked if you were planning on going. Close enough."

I replayed the conversation in my head. Could it be true? Could he have been asking me to the dance?

I groaned. "It doesn't matter now. I told him I wasn't going. I blew it."

"It's not too late. Go find him and tell him you're going."

I shook my head. "I don't even have a dress, and it's next week."

"Just go shopping this weekend. It's not a big deal."

My grandma was coming this weekend. But maybe I could go shopping tonight. I paused, thinking about it. I supposed that was possible. But I was in such a bad mood because of this newspaper thing. Did I really want to go to a dance, even if Cole would be there?

Lin started pulling me up and out of my seat. "You should go find Cole before he leaves the school."

"But why bother?" I croaked.

"Because the newspaper isn't everything, and you need one thing to go right today."

Once again, Lin was spot-on with her advice. "Okay."

Her face lit up. "You'll do it?"

"Yeah."

"Okay, you'd better hurry." She practically pushed me out the doorway.

I didn't know where Cole was, but he'd only been gone a couple of minutes, so he couldn't have gone far. I turned a corner into the next hall and saw him in the distance, stopped at his locker.

My nerves prickled as I walked toward him. What if Lin was wrong? What if Cole had only been asking because he was curious? Or because he wanted to make sure I *wouldn't* be there? Or because he was thinking about writing an article about the dance? There were so many options, and just following Lin's assumption could end in deep and painful humiliation.

When I was writing an article, doing research, or interviewing someone, I felt super confident. Why did the thought of talking to Cole about the dance make me feel like I was being chased by a bear? I took a deep breath and told my heart to chill out. Everything would be fine.

An idea occurred to me. I'd pretend I was interviewing him for a newspaper article. I'd trick my nerves. That would work!

I dashed down the length of the hall until I reached his locker.

"Hey, Cole!"

He turned around, surprised, and then flashed me that big smile.

Oh no. Here it was. The chased-by-a-bear feeling.

I gave him an awkward smile back. And then totally forgot what I was going to say.

"Um, did you want something?" he asked at my weird and socially unacceptable silence.

"Um, about, you said before, um, your question."

His brow furrowed at the word salad coming out of my mouth. "Are you talking about the dance?"

I raised a finger in the air. "Yes! That! Um, I am going after all."

His face brightened. "Oh, great! I'll see you there, then."

And with that he closed his locker and walked away.

The conversation had actually been pretty easy, though I still didn't know what it meant. But at least it had temporarily taken the sting off the horrible advisor news.

Now that I thought about it, things weren't so bad. Maybe Lin was right and this would only be a short-term problem. Everything would work out okay.

With a smile and a hop in my step, I headed down the corridor toward the main door. I had about twenty minutes before the late bus came to pick up kids from after-school activities. So I took my time, running my hand along the lockers and smiling at everyone who walked by.

Until I came to the office.

Principal Pickford was standing in the doorway talking to Cee, and she looked upset. Her arms were crossed, and though I couldn't make out their words, her voice seemed extra high and *off*.

I picked up the pace. He wasn't getting mad at her about my cafeteria article, was he? It wasn't her fault. It had been my decision to write it.

I reached them and wrapped my hand protectively around Cee's arm. "What's going on?"

She turned to me, her eyes shiny and wet. "He's killing the Red Club!"

My head snapped toward Mr. Pickford. "What? Why?"

"I'm only following the rules in the handbook. It clearly states that each club needs an advisor, and the Red Club has been operating with students alone."

"So we'll get one," I said quickly. I was already running through teachers in my mind, thinking about who might say yes.

"Each club also needs approval from me," he said, pointing a thumb at his chest. "We got complaints about the Red Club. There are unhappy students and therefore unhappy parents."

"Who?" I asked, baffled by the thought.

"You know I can't tell you that. But between the complaints and the fact that you've been operating against the rules—"

"We didn't know about the rule!" Cee pleaded. "No one warned us or anything."

He put up his hand. "It was an unapproved club. I'm sorry, but those are the rules."

CHAPTER 8

CEE SENT OUT A GROUP TEXT CALLING for an emergency meeting of the Red Club at her house—eighth-grade leadership only. Just like we didn't have a club president but Cee ran things, we didn't have officers but we had the eighth-grade girls who came every week. And that was me, Cee, Stella, and Camille.

We settled onto the rug in Cee's room, which looked more like an executive's office than a thirteen-year-old's bedroom. She had sleek, modern furniture and framed posters with inspirational quotes. A glass-top desk was the centerpiece of the room, with a sleek silver laptop and an overly complicated-looking filing system.

Cee placed some snacks in the center of our circle and got everyone up to speed with Principal Pickford's decision.

Stella shook her head of long, red curls. "What are we going to do?"

"I honestly don't know," Cee said. "But I don't want to give up without a fight."

"Your room is awesome, Cee," Camille said. "How about we have the club meetings here every week? The school can't shut the club down if it meets off school property."

Cee shook her head. "We can't. My mom works from home. It was hard enough to convince her to let this one meeting happen."

"Plus," I said, "the point is that the Red Club is an open club at school for any girl who needs it. Can you imagine some shy sixth grader showing up at an eighth grader's house?"

"I wouldn't have done that," Stella admitted. "And I'm really confident."

"We noticed," Camille said under her breath.

Cee plucked a piece of lint off the rug. "Having the club meet somewhere else changes the feel of it. There is something safe about the school library. It feels comfortable."

"We obviously have some sort of advisor," Stella pointed out. "Someone makes sure the locker belongs to the club every year and doesn't get assigned to a student. And the combination never changes."

Cee wrapped one of her braids around her finger. "And when supplies are running low, they magically reappear. I know a few of us have donated stuff. But items have also appeared without any of us knowing who did it."

"And we have the library automatically booked every Wednesday afternoon," Camille added.

I reached out to the bowl of chips and grabbed a handful. "Maybe our secret helper would agree to be our advisor."

"But we don't even know who it is," Cee said. "No one has ever known."

Stella frowned. "And if there was a period fairy god-mother, wouldn't she have come forward and helped us?"

"Only if she *could* help," I said. "Her hands are probably tied like Ms. Bhatt's with the newspaper drama."

"It doesn't matter anyway," Cee said sadly. "There's still the problem of the complaints."

I hated this. Someone complained, and the club

was taken away from the rest of us? What about all the girls who needed the club? Were they less important than one angry parent?

Tears pricked the corner of my eyes. "Why would they do this to us?"

"It's so unfair," Camille said.

Cee shook her head in disgust. "Think about all the girls who got support from this club over the years. Girls who are off to college right now."

I added, "And think about all the little girls in elementary who won't have this club when they need it. Between this, the newspaper changes, and the dress code, I don't even recognize Hawking Middle right now."

Stella coughed gently into her hand. "I totally agree with everything you're all saying, but I just don't want these bad feelings to poison the dance next week."

"Stella, really?" Camille snapped. "Is that important right now?"

"It is!" Stella's cheeks turned as red as her hair. "I worked really hard. The committee worked hard. They've taken away our leggings and cute tank tops. They've taken away our club. We can't let them ruin this dance, too."

When she worded it that way, I got kind of fired

up. I'd been thinking about skipping the dance, even after the conversation with Cole, because I couldn't imagine being in the mood to laugh and celebrate. But now I wanted to go. I wouldn't let all these changes ruin my plans for an amazing night.

"She's right," I said. "Even when terrible things are happening, we should still be allowed to have some fun and forget."

Cee stood and brushed potato-chip crumbs off her jeans. "And I still need to run my business. Emergency meeting is adjourned. For now."

I'd been texting Ava all afternoon, but she hadn't responded because of practice. She usually couldn't respond to texts until nighttime. I knew she wasn't going to the dance. She had a practice that night— shocker. But I was at least hoping for some best-friend dress-shopping advice. I wasn't about to bring that up in this meeting with the fashion police in attendance.

Instead I texted my mom:

Could you take me dress shopping? I'm going to my first school dance.

She quickly texted back in all caps:

YES! I THOUGHT YOU'D NEVER ASK! GIRLS' NIGHT!!!!

A little smile lifted the corner of my mouth. At least one person would be happy today.

CHAPTER 9

MY MOM WAS THE QUEEN OF SKIRTS and dresses. I supposed she had to have some for work, but she even wore them when she could've worn sweats. I'd never been into dresses or fashion. My jeans and hoodies were comfy, and I liked them just fine. I was happier saving my money for more books or a new laptop. But apparently my mother had been waiting my whole life for this moment. She was smiling so wide, she looked like a demented clown.

"If none of the stores at the mall have anything,

there are a couple little shops I know that we can try," she said, guiding the car into a parking spot.

I didn't really want to make a big production out of it. The first dress in the first store that didn't look horrible was fine by me.

She killed the engine, then put her finger in the air like she'd thought of something else. "You'll need shoes, too."

"Oh yeah. I guess I can't wear my favorite purple sneakers to a dance." I lifted my foot up to show them off. "Unless I get a purple dress and it matches."

Mom's mouth dropped open, aghast.

"Just kidding," I said with a smirk. "I'll get new shoes. But no heels! Ballet flats will be fine."

"What about a short heel, and we'll get ice cream on the way home?"

"You run a tough bargain, lady," I said, but I agreed. First, because *ice cream*. Second, because if the shoes were really uncomfortable, I could always kick them off and dance barefoot.

We breezed through the first store, a small boutique. Mom dismissed everything as "too casual."

"You know this isn't prom, right?" I said, trying to keep up with her fast stride on the way to the next store.

"Yes, Riley. I'm not looking for a gown, but I don't want anything too blah either."

"Not too blah," I repeated with a giggle. "Maybe that's what we should say to the salesperson."

The next stop was a department store, which had a much larger selection. We headed toward the juniors section and started flipping through the racks.

I held up a knee-length orange dress.

"Not with your skin tone," she said.

Um, okay.

Mom held up a sparkly gold dress with sequins.

"Sequins? Do you know me at all?" I snarked.

Mom laughed. "So why the hurry?" she asked. "It's unlike you to be spontaneous like this. You always plan things ahead."

"It was a last-minute decision," I said as nonchalantly as I could. I flipped past four dresses in a row that had spaghetti straps—something that wouldn't pass our new dress code.

"You've never been to one of the middle school dances before. Can Ava make it to this one?"

"Of course not," I said, rolling my eyes. "She has practice, like always."

"Then why are—" Mom's eyes widened. "Did a boy ask you?"

I froze, my hand on a hanger. "I don't know."

Her brow furrowed. "What do you mean, you don't know?"

"He didn't ask me to, like, go with him. But he asked if I was going to be there."

"And is that why you decided to go?" she asked, grinning ear to ear.

"Yes," I admitted with a sigh, "but please don't make a big deal out of it."

Mom dropped the dress she was holding and flailed her hands in the air. "Oh my goodness! What's his name? Does he come from a good family?"

"Mom," I interrupted. "We're not getting married. He just asked if I was going to be there. Could you please chill out?" Her excited questions were kind of cute. Though it slightly annoyed me that Mom never got that excited over my investigative reports. But she was starting to make me nervous. What if it *was* a date? What if it was a bigger deal than I thought?

"Sure, honey," she agreed through a huge smile. "I'll be chill and relaxed. I'll be chillaxed."

"No," I said. I hated when she tried to be a "cool mom," but I couldn't help but smile at the same time.

"What?" she said innocently. "I'm just saying it's all good. It's chillastic."

"Mom, stop."

"The whole rest of the night is going to be a chilla-thon."

I hung my head and tried to bury my face between two hangers.

"What about this one?" Mom asked.

I peeked out and then stood up straight. She held up a blue dress that looked, well, perfect. I loved the color. It had cap sleeves and was knee-length, so I wouldn't run into dress-code problems. It wasn't too fancy or too casual. It was just right. Like the Goldilocks of dresses.

"I'll try it on!" I said, grabbing the dress in excitement.

The fluorescent lighting in the dressing room didn't do me—or anyone—any favors. I looked ghastly pale, except for the two zits that the bright lights seemed to amplify like a magnifying glass. I didn't understand it. These stores wanted to make money, right? They should have used more flattering lighting. Maybe someday when Cee owned her own chain of stores, she'd make that change.

"How does it look?" Mom asked. I could see her feet bouncing in place on the other side of the door.

I took one last glance in the mirror. I thought it looked good. The only problem was that it was a V-neck style and I didn't have much in the boob department. I took a deep breath and stuck my chest out. That looked a little better, but I couldn't walk around holding my breath all night.

"Come on," Mom said. "Let me see."

I unlatched the door and let it swing open.

Mom covered her mouth with her hand. "It's gorgeous! You're beautiful!" She pulled me in for a hug, then pushed me away to look me up and down again. "You should get out of those hoodies more often."

"Thanks," I said, ignoring her dig about my daily attire and focusing on the compliment part.

She inspected me for a moment more. "You don't seem happy. Do you want to keep looking? There are plenty more stores."

"No, it's not that." I stared down at my bare feet. "I want the dress. It's just . . . I had a bad day."

She lifted my chin up with her finger to make me look her in the eye. "What happened?"

"The school is all of a sudden going hard on these rules from the handbook. We lost Ms. Bhatt as the newspaper advisor and we're going on 'break' for a while until Principal Pickford writes up new rules. And all these girls lost class time because they were dress-coded, including Ava."

She nodded slowly. "That was the focus of the school committee meeting last night. It's been brewing for a while, but it must seem like it's out of the blue for you students."

"And even worse, the Red Club got shut down." My voice cracked. "Someone complained, and Principal Pickford said we were an illegal club because we didn't have an advisor, but he won't let us *get* an advisor."

She stared down at the floor for a moment. "I know that this Red Club meant a lot to you and you're disappointed. I'm sorry about that."

"Thanks," I muttered.

"But maybe it's time to move on. You've had your monthlies for years now; you don't need that club."

I held in a sigh and turned around. I'd give her my speech about support and sisterhood again, but I'd be wasting my breath. She hadn't gotten it before, and she wouldn't get it now. We were too different. Despite how nice the afternoon had been, she'd never understand me.

"I just think that you should let it go," she said softly.

Something in her voice made me look over my shoulder. "You didn't complain about the club to the school committee or Principal Pickford, did you?"

Her mouth opened, and she looked a little hurt. "No, of course not."

"Did anyone mention the Red Club at the committee meeting?" I asked.

She thought for a moment. "Not the club, no. But a few mothers complained about rules not being enforced. For example, Mrs. Scruggs spoke at length about the dress code and how the administration needs to start taking it seriously and enforcing it so the boys aren't distracted. Apparently, her son has some problems focusing on his work."

Mom made a face, and I joined in—rolling my eyes so hard it hurt. Everyone knew that Brody was failing a bunch of classes, but it had more to do with him not studying or even attempting his homework than seeing a girl's shoulder. But of course his mom, convinced that it couldn't be the fault of her precious angel, blamed the girls. Brody spent most of his time torturing and bullying other students rather than studying, but yeah, it was definitely the leggings' fault.

But still, that wasn't the Red Club. "So no one asked the principal to shut the club down?"

"Not during the school committee meeting. But you have to understand, for every parent who stands up and complains during a public meeting, there are ten more who book time with the principal to complain privately."

That was probably what had happened here. And that person had ruined the Red Club for all of us. I knew Mom didn't approve and thought "talk like that" should be private. But she wouldn't go so far as to get my club shut down, would she? I chewed on my lip. No. No way. Plus, she'd denied it.

I only wished I believed her.

CHAPTER 10

FRIDAY, EVERYONE WAS FREAKING OUT
about the dress code. So many girls had been coded
yesterday and sent home or forced to change. No one
wanted to repeat that mistake, but emotions were
high. Some were afraid; some were angry; almost all
were confused.

I stopped at my locker beside an intense conversation between two seventh graders.

"You're going to get coded," a girl said to her friend,
pointing at her legs.

"My shorts are the same as yours," she said.

"But when you hold your arms down by your side, your fingertips can't be past the end of your shorts, and yours are."

"I've got long arms and short legs! It's not my fault I'm out of proportion!" She buried her face in her hands and stormed off.

This wasn't right. None of it.

I'd read the handbook the night before, to take notes for an article I wanted to write. The dress code was in there to prevent any "disruption of the learning environment." But the only math that girls were focusing on today was arm length and strap width. The dress code itself was the disruption, not a rogue shoulder.

And the boys weren't affected at all. There wasn't anything in the handbook targeting clothing that boys wore. They didn't make spaghetti-strap boy tanks or boy short shorts. (Or if they did, they didn't sell them in the stores I went to.) The boys were all going about their day as normal, casually walking from class to class, studying their notes. And meanwhile the girls were filled with anxiety about whether they'd be sent home because of a centimeter.

I grabbed my usual seat at the far-corner lunch table where Ava and I sat every day. Cee and my other friends had second lunch. Sometimes it made me sad to think about the big group of them, all chatting and having fun. Though Ava seemed to like it being just us at first lunch. She had me all to herself.

But she didn't look too happy now. She walked up to the table with a grimace on her face and slammed her tray down. The lettuce in her salad bounced.

"What's wrong?" I asked.

"It's these jeans." She eased herself down onto the chair. "They're so stiff and hot. I hate them. I miss my leggings."

I popped a grape in my mouth. "Maybe you'll get used to jeans?"

She shook her head. "You don't know what it's like to be my size."

I nodded, knowing it was true. Ava was so short, she needed tiny girl sizes. But her thigh muscles were legit from all those years of gymnastics. So those short, skinny sizes were strangling her muscular legs.

"I just don't feel comfortable," she said. "I can barely concentrate in class."

"Maybe try some khakis?" I suggested.

She stabbed a cherry tomato with her fork. "I don't own any. My mom will have to take me shopping. But I don't know when. You know what my schedule is like."

"Yeah." Man, did I know. She brought it up all the

time. But still, I understood. "If they were going to suddenly start enforcing these rules, it would have been nice to give us some warning."

"I know, right?" She used her knife and fork to cut up the slices of chicken on the top of her salad into tiny cubes.

Vanita, the other girl at our table who'd been dress-coded, sat down beside us with a friend. She shared a knowing nod with Ava, like two girls who'd been through something together.

"Missing your leggings?" she asked.

"More than you know," Ava said.

"Me too," Vanita said with a sigh.

"Hey, so, my grandmother is visiting this weekend," I said quickly before I forgot. I'd been meaning to bring this up earlier.

"Ouch," Ava said with a wince. "Like this week wasn't rough enough already."

"Why is that bad?" Vanita asked, curious.

"Riley's mom can be kind of . . . formal," Ava explained. "But her grandmother is that times a thousand. And then the two of them argue the whole time they're together."

I nodded in agreement. Ava knew. Over the years, she'd been around for so many of those visits, and she'd witnessed the weird passive-aggressiveness between my mom and grandmother. Ava had always been there for me during those visits. And I knew she'd be there for me now.

"So, can I sleep over Saturday night?" I asked. "It would be nice to get out of my house."

Ava grimaced. "Sorry. I'm away at a comp this weekend."

I heaved a sigh. I'd really been hoping for that break.

"Speaking of gymnastics," she said, her face brightening, "in a couple weeks I'm having a little get-together at my house with some of the girls, and I want you to be there. It's a Wednesday, our afternoon off from the gym. Will you come?"

"Me? Why?" I'd never hung out with her gymnastics friends before, though I'd chatted with them a little bit when I went to cheer her on at competitions. The girls were all from other towns. They'd probably be talking about gymnastics stuff I knew nothing about. It was nice of Ava to include me, but she really didn't have to.

"Well . . ." She gazed over at the other girls at the table to make sure they weren't listening anymore. "If no one from town comes to my party, they'll think I have no friends."

And there it was. She wasn't inviting me to be nice. She was inviting me to make herself look good.

I took a bite of my sandwich and chewed it while I thought. "That sounds cool. I'll let you know."

Ava frowned, causing a little line to form between her blond eyebrows. "Why not let me know now? You won't have a Red Club meeting. What else do you have going on?"

I stared at her blankly, trying to mask how frustrated I was. She hadn't even asked me how I felt about getting my club taken away. Everything was about her. *Her* busy schedule. *Her* gymnastics friends.

"We're not going to accept that the club was shut down," I said. "We're going to try to get it back." I had no idea if that was true. We'd only had one emergency meeting so far. But I wanted to keep my Wednesdays open just in case.

Ava let out an annoyed sigh.

"I'm going to the dance next Friday," I blurted, changing the subject.

Ava's mouth opened in surprise. "You are?"

"Yeah, remember when I texted you a million times yesterday and you didn't respond? That was for dress advice."

She looked down at her fork, hanging in midair.

"Sorry. I had a really bad day, and when I finally came home from the gym, I just went to bed and cried."

Cried? I sat up straighter in my seat. "What happened?"

She pushed her food around a bit on the plate. "Well, first I got dress-coded. That was humiliating. Then I didn't stick the landing off the vault two times in a row, and the girls were laughing behind my back." Her voice got high and tight like she was fighting back tears.

She had somehow turned the conversation back to her again, but my heart clenched when I thought about those girls laughing at her. Ava was the best, and when the best screwed up, mean people loved it.

I gripped my sandwich tight enough to leave a thumbprint in the bread. "Are those the girls who are going to be at your house?"

"Yeah," she said softly.

I couldn't let Ava face them alone. She needed support. "I'll be there."

She looked up, her eyes grateful and wide. "You will?"

"Definitely. We'll have a great time."

A huge smile spread across her face. "Okay, now tell me about this dress."

CHAPTER 11

GRANDMA SHOWED UP SATURDAY MORNING,
and it took less than an hour for things to get awkward.

"Those jeans are too tight, don't you think?" she
said to my mother, while pointing at me.

"They're called skinny jeans, Grandma," I said. "All
the girls my age wear them."

She shook her head, clucking in disapproval.

Whenever I thought my mom was uptight, getting
a visit from Grandma reminded me that it could have
been way worse.

We were sitting in the living room trying to decide how to spend our day. Mom and Dad liked everyone to go out somewhere because things tended to be less testy if strangers were around. Grandma never wanted to "cause a scene." But Grandma liked to stay in the house and "catch up," which basically meant sit around and talk.

Thankfully, Danny had a soccer game. So that would get us out for a couple of hours.

"Everyone has to come watch me," Danny said. "Remember, Mom, you missed last weekend's game."

"Yes, but I sold a house during that time," Mom said, rearranging the same throw pillows she'd already straightened.

"You wouldn't miss out on anything if you chose to be a mother rather than a real estate agent," Grandma muttered.

Dad and I shared a look that said, *Here we go.*

"I *am* a mother," Mom said. "These are my two children—Riley and Danny. Maybe you've met them?"

"You know what I mean," Grandma said with a huff. "I'll never understand how you can choose work over these sweet children."

Dad put his hand on Mom's knee and gave it a squeeze. Her face was turning a deep shade of red, like she was holding her breath for too long.

Grandma ruffled Danny's hair. "So how long do we have before this soccer game?"

"One hour," Mom said through gritted teeth.

Grandma smiled at me. "Do you think that's enough time for presents?"

Before I could answer, Danny jumped up from the couch. "Yeah, yeah! Presents!"

Grandma shuffled over to the corner and pulled four wrapped boxes out of her overnight bag. Then she handed one to each of us. We immediately began tearing off the wrapping paper.

Danny got his open first and screamed in delight. "My favorite player!" He held up a soccer jersey from his favorite team, and the last name on the back was the guy he was always talking about.

Dad held up his next. "It's a shoe-polishing kit. Thank you so much." He got up and gave Grandma a quick kiss on the cheek.

"Now you'll look even more handsome and professional at work," Grandma said.

I finally got my box open and gasped. Inside was a beautiful, delicate silver bracelet. "Thank you, Grandma. This is gorgeous."

"Just like you, sweetheart," she replied.

Mom went last, holding up a pair of long gold earrings. "These are beautiful, Mom. Thank you."

Grandma smiled. "I thought you'd look pretty with dangly earrings, rather than the same old studs you wear every day."

Those were the diamond studs my father had given her, but he didn't say a word.

"No one can even see my ears," Mom said. "The studs are comfortable. They don't get caught in my hair like longer earrings would."

"Well, it's time for a haircut anyway," Grandma said flatly. "You're too old for that length."

That length was just a bit below her shoulders. Lots of moms had longer hair. I didn't want Mom to cut her hair super short like Grandma's. It was pretty the way it was. But from the flames in my mom's narrowed eyes, I didn't think she'd be rushing out to the salon anytime soon.

"Well, thank you for the gift," Mom said, keeping her voice even. "The earrings are beautiful, and I'll save them for a special occasion when I wear my hair up."

Grandma's response was a small grunt and a change of subject. "I'm going to head into the kitchen and make sure you have all the ingredients for me to make my lasagna for dinner."

"Oh, I'm cooking tonight," Dad said. "Don't you worry about that."

"Nonsense," Grandma said. "I'm sure you have much more important things to do than slave away in the kitchen."

In addition to never having moved on from 1950s fashion sense, Grandma had weird feelings about men and women splitting household chores. The fight after she'd found out Dad did his own laundry still echoed somewhere in the house's walls.

This time it was Mom's turn to squeeze Dad's knee.

"Lasagna sounds lovely," Dad said.

"Riley, why don't you help your mother and me with dinner?" Grandma asked, but it wasn't a suggestion.

I looked at Mom, who was staring down at her hands.

Sometimes it was easier to go along than to fight it.

Grandma's cooking was always amazing. And she gave great presents. But I'd have traded it all for peace. Just once, I'd have liked her visit to not end with my mom in tears.

CHAPTER 12

I SPENT MOST OF SUNDAY HIDING OUT in my room writing an article about the dress code. First, it kept me away from any house drama that might have been going on. And second, it made me feel better to get my feelings down on paper. I hadn't been able to talk about the dress code all weekend. Grandma definitely would have been Team No Leggings. So it felt good to let it all out on my laptop.

Monday morning I rushed right to Principal Pickford's office. Miss Nancy must have been somewhere else in the school, but his door was open, so I tiptoed in. He was typing quickly on his computer, ignoring the ringing phone and the fact that his glasses were about to slip right off his nose.

"Um, excuse me, Principal Pickford?" I said warily.

He glanced at me and took a moment to push up his glasses. "Yes, Riley?"

"I know you said you'd let us know when the next newspaper meeting would be, but I wrote an article that's pretty timely that I think should go up on the site, and I'd like to e-mail it to you."

"Okay," he said, barely looking up from his computer. "But I prefer to read printed copies. You can just toss it on my inbox. I'll read it when I can." He motioned toward a basket stacked high with piles of papers and file folders.

Since this was my first time submitting an article to him, I'd been prepared for that just in case and pulled out a printed copy of the article. I carefully placed it on top of the pile. Who knew when he'd get to it? But at least I was trying. It felt better than doing nothing.

I backed out of the office and found Ava in the hall.

"How was your comp?" I asked.

She shrugged. "Okay, I guess. How was your grandma's visit?"

"Imagine it in your head for a minute." I paused. "Now make it ten times worse."

She winced. "Sorry."

I shrugged like it was nothing. But it wasn't nothing. It was hard to watch Grandma and Mom bicker so much. And it made me worry that when I grew up, that would be me and Mom. I didn't want us to end up like that.

As if she could read my mind, Ava said, "Don't worry. You and your mom will never be like that."

My heart swelled. Ava knew me so well. I was about to give her a huge hug, but Cee rushed up and grabbed my arm.

"Ready to go?" Cee asked breathlessly.

"Where are you guys going?" Ava asked.

"To try to get an advisor for the Red Club," I explained. Cee and I had come up with a plan over text the day before. "We have to find a way to bring it back."

Something flashed across Ava's eyes.

"Good luck," she said in a small voice.

Cee practically pulled my arm out of its socket dragging me down the hallway. "We only have a couple minutes before the bell is going to ring."

Ms. Bhatt was organizing her desk when we burst in.

"Ms. Bhatt!" I called, out of breath. "We need to ask you something."

She flashed a smile. "Sure, girls. What's up?"

Cee straightened her shoulders. "We want you to be the advisor for the Red Club."

Her smile fell.

"Before you say no," Cee rushed on, "let us tell you about it. The club is so supportive and wonderful. It has created friendships and bonds."

"And since Principal Pickford took the newspaper away from you, you'd have the time," I added. "It's only one afternoon a week."

"You would help so many girls," Cee said.

Ms. Bhatt put her hand up to stop us. "Girls, girls. I would never say no. I've always admired the Red Club. I wish I'd had something like it growing up in India."

"So you'll be our advisor?" I practically screeched with happiness.

"No," she said sadly.

"Why not?" Cee asked.

"Because I already suggested the idea and got turned down."

I staggered back a step. "What?"

"When I heard about the club getting shut down,

I approached Principal Pickford and told him that I'd love to be the club's advisor." She glanced at the doorway and lowered her voice. "But the club not having an advisor was only a technicality, not the main problem."

"What's the main problem?" Cee asked.

"The complaints," I said.

Ms. Bhatt nodded.

"So even if we got an advisor, we wouldn't get our club back," Cee said, putting it all together.

Ms. Bhatt gazed down at the floor. "I believe not."

The bell rang. I had Ms. Bhatt for homeroom, so I could stay where I was, but Cee would have to rush off.

"What are we going to do?" Cee said, her voice low and discouraged. "I don't want to give up."

An idea formed in my brain. I'd tackled plenty of investigations in this school before. . . . "Maybe the key to getting the club back is uncovering the identity of the secret complainer."

Cee flashed a wicked grin. "If only we knew an awesome investigative reporter."

That night at dinner, I stared down at my enchilada in dread. It was my turn next in the Dunne Family Dinner Game, and I couldn't think of anything to say. My day had been one frustration after another. I'd given Principal Pickford a new article, but I didn't think he'd read it anytime soon. I'd tried to get an advisor for the Red Club and found out that wouldn't work. Everything I'd tried had failed. And I didn't really want to say that the thing I was looking forward to was investigating secret complainer suspects. Especially when my own mom was on the list.

"Riley?" Dad said, poking me lightly with his elbow.

I hadn't realized Danny had finally stopped talking. I thought he'd go on forever about that dodgeball game. I had nothing positive to say about today, but I could think of the second half of my turn. There was one other idea I'd gotten. A work-around that I could use until the newspaper started up again.

I wiped my mouth with a napkin. "I didn't have a great thing happen today, but I do have something to look forward to. I've been thinking about starting a blog."

"A blog," Mom repeated. "What for?"

"For my articles that Principal Pickford won't publish. That way the writing isn't wasted. Instead of going up on the school's newspaper site, I can just put it up on my own site."

"How would that work, exactly?" Dad asked.

I chewed on my lower lip for a moment. I hadn't thought it through completely. It was a new idea.

"I don't really know," I admitted. "I'll have to do a lot of research, figure out how to set a blog up and design it. And after I post my articles, I'll have to figure out how to let people know how to find them."

Mom put down her fork and put on her serious face. "Honey, that seems like a lot of work. You don't have time for that."

The little bit of hope I'd had deflated like a popped balloon.

Dad said, "Maybe you can start a blog next summer when you're not busy with school."

And write about what? I thought. All the big stories were happening now. I stared down at my soggy enchilada. I officially had nothing to look forward to. The Red Club was gone. The newspaper was on hold. Everything that I cared about was in disarray.

"I don't know how long Principal Pickford is going to take to restart the newspaper," I said. "I'm going to miss writing. It's . . . it's a part of me."

"Well, no one said you couldn't *write*," Mom said. "I just don't want you starting this whole blog business."

"What about a short story?" Dad suggested. "I'd love to read it. Especially if it's a mystery."

"Yeah, maybe," I said, poking my fork at the cheesy mess that used to be an enchilada. But the only mystery I was interested in ended with me getting my life back.

CHAPTER 13

WEDNESDAY, I WOKE UP WITH THE excitement I usually did on Red Club mornings. It was my favorite weekday, knowing I'd get to hang with my friends after school, laugh, and help people. It took a full minute after my alarm went off for me to remember. The club was gone.

But it had been two days since I'd submitted my article to Principal Pickford. I thought that was enough time to check in.

I stopped at the office as soon as I got to school.

Miss Nancy looked up from her desk. "Good morning, Riley. How can I help you?"

"I was hoping to talk to Principal Pickford. I gave him an article for the newspaper on Monday, and I was wondering if he'd read it yet."

Miss Nancy grimaced. "He's been very busy lately—"

But just as she began, his door opened, and he barged out with a stack of papers in his hands. He plopped them down on her desk and said, "I need to finish those interviews for the new art teacher. Book them all for tomorrow, back to back."

Miss Nancy barely had time to nod before her phone started ringing.

Mr. Pickford turned around and startled, not realizing I was standing there. "Oh, good morning, Riley."

"Hi, Principal Pickford," I began. "I see that you're busy, but I was wondering if you had a chance to read my article?"

"I did, actually," he said.

My heart sped up. I hadn't expected that. I'd thought the paper would sit on his desk until it biodegraded.

"It was well written," he said. "You have a gift with words. But it's not really what I'm looking for. Instead of an opinion piece, write the facts. Detail the rules of the dress code and what will happen if students break them. I'll publish that."

I held back a sigh. So he just wanted me to copy the paragraph from the old handbook. That wasn't writing. That wasn't what I'd joined the newspaper to do. But I didn't talk back or complain. I had a bigger mission this morning. Ms. Bhatt had said that getting an advisor wouldn't help. But maybe if I tried in person. *Begged.*

"I was also hoping to talk to you about the Red Club again," I began.

"Riley, I—"

I interrupted, "I've been doing some research and talking with people, and we would have no problems getting an advisor."

"It's not just that," he said. "We had complaints."

"I realize that, but if we're following the rules—"

He cut in. "Parents think these things need to be discussed at home."

"But that's part of why the Red Club is so great. Not all girls get that support at home." *Like me,* I thought. I wanted my club back. I needed this.

He looked at me with something like sympathy. "Riley, I understand why you're upset. Believe me, I do. But I had upset parents to deal with too. Parents who had good points about the Red Club."

"Could you tell me who complained? Maybe I could talk to them and help them understand."

He shook his head. "You know I can't do that."

Miss Nancy pulled the phone away from her face and covered the mouthpiece. "Mrs. Scruggs is on line two. Brody got a test back that she feels was unfairly graded, and she's demanding to speak with you."

Pickford rubbed his hands over his face. "I'll take it in my office."

The morning dragged by. I didn't know if it was the new dress code or what, but a lot of girls seemed sad. Not just me.

Paige came up to me in the hall between classes. "Is the Red Club meeting anywhere today?"

"It's shut down," I said. "You heard about that, right?"

"Well, yeah, but I thought you'd find another way. Like maybe we could meet somewhere else? I really need the club today." Her eyes were rimmed with red.

"Are you okay?" I asked.

"Physically, yeah. But I've been feeling really . . ." She stopped and looked around, like she just remembered we were talking in the middle of the hall with a bunch of kids walking past. "It's fine. I'll go to a friend's house and talk it out there."

My stomach felt sick. Here was a girl who needed our support, and we couldn't be there for her.

"If it doesn't work out at your friend's house, you can always text me," I said. "Anytime."

She nodded and walked away, head down.

At lunchtime I headed into the cafeteria and sat at my usual spot. Ava had left math early to head to the bathroom and still wasn't there yet.

Julia was sitting a few tables away with Hazel, the two of them laughing. If it hadn't been for the Red Club, they probably wouldn't have become friends, but now they had each other. As they laughed, my heart warmed. The Red Club had done that.

And now it was gone.

I had to investigate. Maybe if I could figure out the identity of the secret complainer, I could use my super-skill on them. I'd tell them my side, explain how important the Red Club was, and get them to change their mind. But first I had to figure out who the secret complainer was. And I knew exactly who I wanted to talk to.

I left my seat and walked over to Julia's table.

"Hey, girls!" I said.

Julia smiled, and Hazel gave me a big wave.

I coughed into my hand. "So, um, Julia, how is your mom adjusting to living in a new town?"

She shrugged. "Pretty well, I guess. She doesn't really have friends yet. She's busy with work and fixing up our new house. But she likes it here."

"Did she go to the school committee meeting?" I asked.

"I . . . don't think so."

"It was last Wednesday night," I said.

Julia tilted her head to the side. "Why do you want to know?"

Uh-oh. What could I say? *Because I think your mom could be the secret complainer who ruined everything for everyone?*

I plastered on a fake smile. "Oh, because my mom goes to those meetings. It could be a good way for your mom to meet people."

"Oh, well, I'll let her know," she said slowly with a slightly confused look on her face.

"Cool," I said. "Um, enjoy the rest of lunch."

As I walked away, I heard Hazel whisper, "Weird."

I returned to my seat and put my face in my hands. So awkward. I was definitely a better writer than interrogator. I focused on eating my lunch, but halfway through, Ava's seat was still empty. Super weird. Even though it was against the rules, I slid my phone out of my pocket and took a peek. Uh-oh. I had one text from her.

I NEED YOU.

The rest of my sandwich sailed into the trash can as I jogged past, headed to the bathroom where Ava had asked me to meet her. I pushed open the door and looked down for feet. There was only one pair, in the middle stall, and I recognized those little white sneakers.

"Ava? You okay?"

"No," she said with a sniffle. "I got my period."

"Oh," I said. *"Oh!"* Her first time! This was what she'd wanted for so long. So why did she seem so sad?

"I don't have . . . anything with me," she said. "And I have a problem."

The stall door slowly swung open, and Ava came out. Her eyes were wet. She'd been crying. She turned around, and I saw a small stain on her brand-new khakis.

Well, it was good that I'd worn a T-shirt under my hoodie again. I pulled the sweatshirt over my head and handed it to her. "No big deal. Wrap this around your waist. We'll get new pants and some pads from the Red Club locker and you'll be good to go."

"I'm sorry," she said.

"It's no problem. Just give the hoodie back to me whenever. That's what friends are for."

This only made her sob harder for some reason.

I grabbed her arm. "Okay, let's visit the locker."

Only a minute later, we stood in front of the infamous locker number one. I twirled the dial, spinning past the combination numbers, and opened it with a dramatic flair. This was her first time, after all. I had to make it special.

But then I was confused.

The locker was empty.

"Where's the stuff?" Ava asked, her voice cracking.

"I—I don't know," I stammered. "I guess when they shut the club down, they had to clear the locker out."

Ava's eyes widened with panic. "What am I going to do?"

I wasn't due for another couple of weeks, so I had nothing in my backpack. I was sure some girl would, but we couldn't exactly wait for lunch to end and go up asking one by one until we hit tampon bingo.

"You can go to the nurse," I said. "If you ask her, I'm sure she has supplies."

"But I don't want to ask," Ava said. "I wanted to just quietly get something from the locker."

"Ms. Owens is nice," I said. "There's no reason to be embarrassed."

"I know I *shouldn't* feel embarrassed, but I still do," she said, tears welling up in her eyes again. "It's my first time. I don't know what I'm doing."

"Okay, I'll go to the nurse," I offered. "I'll get you something."

"And what about my pants?"

I hesitated. I didn't know if the nurse could do anything about that.

"I'm going home," Ava cried. "I need my mom."

After school, I went next door to Ava's house to see how she was doing. Her mom told me she was up in her room. I walked up the stairs like I had a thousand times before and gently knocked on the bedroom door.

A muffled voice responded, "Come in."

I opened the door and poked my head inside. Ava was lying in bed, legs curled up, eyes rimmed red. When she saw it was me, she pushed herself up to sitting.

"You came over to check on me?" she asked through sniffles.

"Of course," I said, easing myself down onto the edge of the bed. "You're my best friend."

Her face scrunched up, like she was going to start crying again.

"Did your mom help you out?" I asked.

"Yeah, but I have questions that she doesn't know the answer to. And you wouldn't know either. Like, gymnast stuff."

"Can you text the other girls from your gym?" I asked.

She made a face. "We're not close like that."

I thought for a minute. "There's a girl in Red Club on the swim team and one who does competitive cheerleading. Oh, and a ballerina! Maybe they could help?"

"But there's no more Red Club!" Ava cried.

"They would still be nice to you. I could give you their names—"

Ava interrupted, "And, what, I'd walk up to them in the hall and ask how to keep a tampon string from showing when you're wearing a leotard? It's not the same."

She was right. She could've easily asked these questions during a club meeting. But without the club . . .

"You know, I never understood why you needed that club so much." Ava wiped her eyes. "I didn't get why it was such a big deal. And now that I need it, it's gone."

"It's okay," I said, brushing the hair off her face. "First off, we're going to get it back. And second, I have something that might cheer you up."

I leaned down and unzipped my backpack. Then I handed my present to Ava, who gave me a little smile in return.

"A Snickers," she said. "My favorite. Want to share?"

I grinned. "Absolutely!"

By the time I went to bed that night, I'd gotten tons of text updates from Cee, Stella, and Camille. They'd heard from a bunch of girls from sixth to eighth grade who were upset because it was our first Wednesday without the club. A few girls had gotten together here and there at one another's houses, but it wasn't the same. It was fractured. The grades stuck together; friends stuck together. What had been great about Red Club was that there were no cliques. No one was left out. That wouldn't happen if we were broken up into a bunch of tiny Red Clubs meeting in various places.

And some girls couldn't get to any meetings at all. It was easy to stay after school and meet in the library. The late bus could bring the girls home just like after any other school club. But they had a harder time getting to other locations. We needed to meet at school to make it work. Which meant we needed Mr. Pickford to change his mind. But I'd tried talking to him. I'd tried getting an advisor. I'd tried begging. Nothing had worked.

I had to figure out who the secret complainer was. And fast.

CHAPTER 14

"YOUR MOM IS STILL WORKING FROM home, right?" I asked Cee on our way out of school Thursday.

"Yeah, why?"

"Think I could come over and ask her some questions for my investigation?"

Cee thought for a moment. "Yeah. If you bring cookies."

I giggled. "Done."

Julia's mom hadn't been at the school committee meeting. That didn't completely rule her out, because she could have met with Pickford privately. But I had hit a dead end with her. The next person on my list of suspects would be a little more difficult to investigate. Mainly because she was my own mother. I'd already asked her if she'd complained about the club, and she'd denied it. But I needed to be sure.

There was another mom I knew who went to all the meetings, and she loved talking to me. And that was why, later that afternoon, I stood at Cee's front door with a plate of freshly baked gluten-free cookies. Well, freshly bought, but whatever.

"If it isn't my second favorite girl from Hawking Middle," Mrs. Butler said, opening the door. "Come on in. Cynthia told me you wanted to talk some things out."

Cee and her mom were really close, and Cee told her everything. So I knew Mrs. Butler would be up on all the details of the school drama.

She poured us three glasses of lemonade, and we sat in the living room on their puffy couch, munching cookies.

"What do you want to know, honey?" Mrs. Butler asked, leaning back against the cushions.

"I'm trying to figure out who complained about the Red Club and got it shut down. I was thinking maybe

Julia's mom, but she wasn't at the school committee meeting."

"Okay . . . ," Mrs. Butler said.

I took a deep breath. "But my mom *was* at the meeting."

Mrs. Butler nodded once. "Yes, she was."

"So . . . did she . . . complain about the club?" I asked.

Mrs. Butler frowned. "Why are you asking me? Why don't you just ask her?"

I stared down at the cookie in my hand. "I did. And she said she didn't complain. But . . ."

"You don't know if you believe her," Mrs. Butler filled in.

I nodded, and my cheeks reddened with shame. This had seemed like a good idea, but now that I was here, investigating my own mother, I felt guilty.

"Also Mrs. Scruggs," I blurted quickly. "I'm also curious about her."

Mrs. Butler blew out an exaggerated breath. "Well, Mrs. Scruggs has a lot to say at every meeting, including this one. But she didn't mention the Red Club and neither did your mother. This last meeting was intense. There was a lot of talk about the dress code and enforcing the handbook. But I don't remember anyone specifically mentioning your club. Sorry, girls."

I felt a wave of relief, but then also frustration. I was no closer to figuring out the identity of the secret complainer than when I'd walked through the door.

Mrs. Butler looked from Cee to me. "Girls, it's not just one person. What's happening at your school is a cumulative effect."

I scrunched my face up. "A what?"

"Things build up." She glanced around the room, eventually settling her eyes on the glass of lemonade in front of her. "See this glass? It's only half full, right?"

I nodded.

"Cynthia, put a bit of your lemonade in there," she ordered.

"Just pour it in?" Cee asked.

Mrs. Butler nodded. "Go on."

Cee poured some lemonade from her glass into her mom's glass.

"Now you, Riley," she said.

I poured some of mine in too. The lemonade was now dangerously close to the top of the glass.

"Again, Cynthia," she said.

Cee gave her an unsure look but did as she was told. The lemonade spilled over the rim and onto the coffee table.

"Now, whose fault was that?" Mrs. Butler asked.

"Was it Cynthia, who poured first? Or Riley, who poured on top of that? Or Cynthia, who went back to pour again?"

"It was all of us," I said, suddenly understanding.

"It builds up," she repeated. "Whether that's poured lemonade or complaints. It builds up."

"So stopping one person from complaining won't help because there are so many other people piling on?" Cee said.

Mrs. Butler asked, "What if it *is* Julia's mom? Or Mrs. Scruggs? Let's say you find out for sure. Then what will you do?"

I jutted my chin out. "Talk to them. Change their mind."

"Then beg them to call Pickford and take it all back," Cee added.

Mrs. Butler gave us a look. "Do you really think the principal is going to go back to ignoring most of the handbook again? He's just going to say, 'Forget everything I said this week'? Do you think the school committee would let him do that?"

She was right. He'd never do that. I sank down deeper into the couch.

"Girls, I don't know if you understand how difficult Mr. Pickford's job is."

Cee crossed her arms. "Why are you defending him?"

Mrs. Butler wagged a finger. "I'm not defending. I'm explaining. What do we know? Parents called complaining about the chicken-nuggets newspaper article. Parents complained about the dress code. Someone complained about the Red Club. There are only so many complaints you can listen to before you want to just give up and give in."

When I really thought about it, it must have been tough to get those calls every day. Someone was always mad about something. But you couldn't just give in!

I walked home with my stomach full of cookies and my head spinning. The club. The newspaper. The dress code. It was all connected by a common thread—people complaining. So maybe if we could fix one, we could fix them all? But how? I had to think of a solution that got our club back and would also return the rest of the school to normal.

But that seemed impossible.

After dinner I finished my homework. Then I went up to my room. This was normally when I'd work on a newspaper article. But that was pointless with no newspaper. I felt the urge to write, though. I missed it.

To scratch my writing itch, I tried working on a

short story. A mystery one, so my dad would enjoy reading it. But no matter how I tried to structure the words, it wouldn't work. I had a group of suspects in the story, but I hadn't yet figured out the villain. And without knowing the villain, I couldn't plant the true clues. I needed to know the end before I wrote the beginning, but it wasn't coming together. Writing for the newspaper came more naturally to me. Journalism was based on the five Ws: *who*, *what*, *where*, *when*, and *why*. Just the facts. I didn't like to make it up as I went along.

I needed the newspaper back. I needed the Red Club back. But I was failing at everything I tried to do to help, even investigating the secret complainer.

What else could I do?

CHAPTER 15

FRIDAY NIGHT, MY MOM PULLED UP TO
the front of the school. "Are you sure I can't get out and
take some pictures? Look, Cee is standing there waiting for you. I need some pictures of the both of you. It's
your first dance!"

Terror shot through me. I was nervous enough. I
wasn't in my normal comfy clothes. I'd be expected to
dance at some point, and I was pretty sure I'd look like
a disaster on the dance floor. And Cole was in there
somewhere. I didn't need an awkward Mom moment
on top of it all.

"I promise I'll take pics with my own phone some-time tonight, okay?" I pleaded. "And I'll text them to you."

Mom agreed, but with a disappointed sigh.

I opened the door to get out, and Mom waved at all the girls waiting on the sidewalk. "Have fun! You all look beautiful!"

I shut the door quickly and closed my eyes until she drove away.

"She's gone," Cee said, sidling up to me. "Your power of closing your eyes to make someone disap-pear worked."

I chuckled. "Was it that obvious?"

"My mom was super embarrassing too," Cee admit-ted. "She yelled out the car window that I should make sure the boys keep their hands to themselves."

Cee wore a flowy, pale yellow dress that looked beautiful against her dark skin. She had on a chunky silver necklace that complemented it perfectly.

"You look awesome," I said. "Love the necklace. Was that a Cee Butler original find?"

Cee nodded, adjusting the clasp with her fingers. "Some old lady sold it for a dollar. It was a bit tar-nished and dull, but after a solid polishing, I got it looking just like new!"

I leaned in to take a closer look. "Amazing."

"Your dress is so pretty." Cee tilted her head to the side. "Where did you get it? It looks familiar. I wonder if I tried it on."

I opened my mouth to answer, but Julia dashed up to us with a look of fear in her eyes. "Oh, Riley. Oh no."

"What?" I asked, my heart speeding up.

"Oh no," Cee echoed, staring at something over my shoulder.

Camille ran over as well. From the panicked expressions on the three girls' faces, there was clearly something horrifying coming up behind me. Various possibilities flitted through my mind—werewolf, vampire, rabid fox, serial killer. Nothing else could explain how intensely they feared for me in that moment.

Preparing myself for the worst, I risked a glance over my shoulder and saw . . . Stella. Not Bigfoot on a rampage or a ghost set on revenge. Just Stella, walking this way . . . in my dress.

We were wearing *the same dress*. Though she filled it out differently—better.

"She's going to kill you," Camille whispered. "Like, straight-up murder."

As Stella got closer and realized what I was wearing, her face contorted into anger.

"Didn't you send a pic for the Instagram page?" Camille asked.

I blinked. "The what?"

"The Instagram dance page Stella set up," Cee explained. "Everyone sent her pics of their dresses, and she posted them on the page so no one would buy the same one."

My stomach flipped over. "I didn't know about it. I've never been to a dance before, and I just decided to go to this one last week."

Someone started humming the theme to the movie *Jaws*.

"You're dead," Camille stated flatly, as if it were an undeniable fact.

Stella came right up to me, wordlessly, which was even scarier than yelling, and placed her hands on her curvy hips. To be honest, Stella looked much better in the dress. She'd paired it with long, dangly earrings and silver heels. Her long red hair was held in a complicated updo. And she filled out the top of the chest department a lot better than I did. I had flats— and I wasn't talking about my shoes.

Finally, after what seemed like a year of silence,

she screeched, "Are you out of your mind?"

I rolled my eyes. "It's okay. It's not the Met Ball. You'll live."

"You'll be lucky if I let *you* live," she said between gritted teeth.

I threw my hands up. "It's just a dress!"

All the girls gasped simultaneously, like I'd said the king of all swears or something.

"Just. A. Dress," Stella repeated, enunciating each word separately.

Maybe a different tactic was in order. "Listen, I'm sorry. I only decided to come to the dance at the last minute."

"Go home and change," Stella ordered.

"I—I can't," I stammered. "This is my only dress."

Stella growled like a ferocious animal. "So now *I* have to go home and change. Wonderful." She whipped out her phone. "Let me see if my mom will even come back and pick me up. I know she's not going to. She has plans tonight."

Cee took me by the elbow and led me toward the front door of the school. "Now's your chance," she whispered. "Let's head inside while she's busy with her phone. She won't kill you *in* the school. Too many chaperones and witnesses."

I watched as a boy opened the door and headed inside. The brief moment when the door hung open gave me a glimpse of lights and people. Music boomed until the door closed, muffling the sound again.

A thought dawned on me. Cole was in there somewhere. And he'd see me and Stella in the same dress.

Cee nudged me with her elbow. "Let's go, okay?"

But my feet wouldn't move. I managed an "um."

Cee's forehead creased. "Stella's not *really* going to kill you."

"It's not that."

"Then what?" she asked.

In my rush to explain, a bunch of word vomit came pouring out all at once. "Cole. Same dress. V-neck. Flats."

Cee shook her head. "Slow down and try again."

I took a deep breath and let my thoughts congeal. Cee knew about my raging crush on Cole, and I'd texted her about our awkward dance conversation. She'd understand.

"If Cole sees us both . . . ," I began.

Cee waved her hand. "Boys don't care if two girls are wearing the same dress."

"It's not that." I scuffed my shoe back and forth on the pavement. "It's *how* we wear it. I don't exactly fill it out like Stella does. Compared to her, I look like a little girl playing dress-up. What if Cole sees us both and thinks . . ."

"That you look different from Stella?" Cee said with raised eyebrows. "Who cares? Cole asked if *you* were coming to the dance, not her. He likes *you*."

"You think so?"

"Yeah, and no amount of incredible boobage is going to change that."

"Thanks, Cee." I rested my head on her shoulder for a moment.

She patted it. "Now let's get inside before that incredible boobage comes to kill you."

Between my fear of talking to Cole and my new-found fear of being murdered by Stella, I had my doubts that I would survive this night.

CHAPTER 16

I HAD TO HAND IT TO STELLA AND THE
dance committee. The place looked amazing. Between
the twinkling lights, the cutout leaves, and the stars
hanging from the ceiling, it didn't even look like our
gym. And it didn't smell like it either, thankfully.

Circles of girls from each grade danced to an upbeat
pop song, now and then yelling out an enthusiastic
"woo!" Most of the boys hung by the wall, pretending
to check their phones, but really checking the girls out.
I wasn't quite in the mood to start jumping and dancing. My nerves were still too frazzled. And then they

suddenly got a lot *more* frazzled, because Cole spied me and started heading my way.

"Oh, look who's coming," Cee teased. "I'm going to get some water."

"No!" I pleaded out of the corner of my mouth. "Don't leave me."

"I've got to get a drink," she said. "It's about to get hot in here."

She dashed away, and I made a mental note to yell at her later.

Cole smiled as he got closer. My legs were trembling like cafeteria Jell-O. I started silently screaming at my brain, *THINK OF SOMETHING COOL TO SAY!* He was going to be here any second!

And then he was there, standing right in front of me.

I opened my mouth and said, "Hey." *Really, brain? That's the best you can do?*

"Hey back," he said with a grin.

I could practically feel my cheeks turn red.

"Are you having fun?" I asked. There. An actual question. Brain progress.

"I just got here," he said. "How about you?"

"Um, yeah, I just got here too." I glanced around the gym. "Everything looks fun. Yay, fun!" *Ugh, smooth, Riley!* My face was now officially on fire. It felt like flames of awkwardness were shooting from my cheekbones.

A slow song started, one that I didn't recognize.

"Do you want to dance?" Cole asked.

He held his hand out, and I looked at it like it was some ancient artifact I'd never seen before. *A boy's hand! Fascinating! Let's stare at it for an awkward length of time rather than grab it!*

I tried to talk myself into it. How long was the average song? Four minutes? I could survive that long without bursting into flames. Maybe.

"Uh, Riley? Are you okay?" Whoops. I guess I was staring more than I thought.

"Yes! S-sure," I said, with total confidence and not dorky at all.

I put my hand in his and let him lead me to the center of the dance floor. Only three other couples were slow dancing, and they were *couples* couples. Like, people who were actually dating. Did this mean we were dating? No, we had to discuss that first, right? Was that how it worked?

My mind had gone from blank to overstuffed in a matter of seconds, and I needed to slow it down.

Cole put his hands on my waist, and I put my hands on his shoulders. We started to sort of sway back and forth. I could barely hear the music over the sound of my own heart going absolutely bonkers in my chest. There was no way I was going to survive four minutes like this.

"It stank not having a newspaper meeting this week," Cole finally said.

"Yeah," I agreed. "I miss it."

"I wonder how long Pickford will take to restart it," he said. "A few weeks could mean anything."

"I tried submitting an article about the dress code." I let out a sigh. "Rejected, of course."

He chuckled. "Wow, you must really miss writing if you tried to get him to publish an article when the paper is not even supposed to be running."

I snorted. "You don't even know. I miss it so much, last night I tried writing a short story!"

"How did that go?"

I smirked. "I should stick to nonfiction."

He threw his head back and laughed. As we chatted back and forth, his hands still on my waist, I realized that I wasn't nervous anymore. I was *dancing with Cole* and my face wasn't on fire. Words flowed freely from my brain to my mouth. I was doing this! Maybe I would survive the night after all.

"Riley!" Camille rushed up to us, breathless.

Cole stopped dancing and moved back a bit, ending the moment.

I gave Camille a look that said, *Really? You have to interrupt right now, when I'm having the best four minutes of my life?* A very specific message, but my eyes were good at expression.

Camille looked from me to Cole and back again. "Sorry, but this is an emergency. It's Stella."

"What about her?" I asked. *If this is part of some plan to ruin my night because I accidentally bought the same dress, I swear . . .*

"They won't let her in," Camille said.

"What? Why?" Cole asked.

Camille looked at me for a long moment. "They dress-coded her."

I blinked quickly, not understanding. How was that possible? We had the same dress, and they'd let *me* in.

Cole shook his head. "This whole dress-code thing is so stupid. It was like one day they just decided and gave no warning. And it's so insulting to boys."

My eyes snapped up to his. "What? How?"

"It's saying we're such idiots that we'll be distracted all day if part of a shoulder is showing. Like, no. Give us more credit than that."

I stared at him. I'd never thought of it that way. "You're right. That's totally insulting."

And then I thought about Stella, stuck outside, not allowed into the dance. How she must have been feeling.

I looked up at Cole as I felt our perfect moment slipping away. "I have to go."

"It's okay," he said. "Check on your friend."

Camille led me to the exit, where we were stopped by one of the chaperones. I immediately recognized that pinched-up face. Mrs. Scruggs, Brody's mother. She had newscaster hair that fell in a blunt bob and was hair-sprayed so hard it didn't move when she shook her head.

She stepped between us and the door. "And where do you think you're going?"

I jutted my chin. "Outside to talk to our friend."

She crossed her arms over her pale pink cardigan and fingered the pearls hanging around her neck. "You know the rules. If you leave, you can't come back in."

I didn't know the rules, actually, it being my first dance at all. But I glanced at Camille and she nodded sadly. If I left now, I wouldn't get another dance with Cole. Over Mrs. Scruggs's shoulder, I saw Stella sitting on the steps outside, her face in her hands. Cee was already out there, an arm around her shoulder.

"Well then, I guess the dance is over for us," I said, pushing past Mrs. Scruggs and out the door.

Cee glanced up at us as we approached, and I knew from the look in her eyes that things were not good. Camille sat down on the other side of Stella. I took the lower step, beneath them, and turned to face everyone.

"What happened?" I asked softly.

Stella lifted her face from her hands. Her perfect makeup job was smeared, and strands of red hair fell from her updo. "My mom couldn't come back, so I decided to just head in—same dress and all. But they coded me."

"Why?" Camille asked.

She sniffed. "They said the dress was inappropriate."

I still didn't understand. "But I have the same dress and they let me in."

A single tear slipped down Stella's cheek. "I guess it's not the dress, then. I guess *I'm* inappropriate."

I looked at Cee, whose eyes had narrowed in anger. Camille's face reddened.

Stella continued. "If I wasn't curvy, I'd be inside that dance right now. I can't help my body type."

"You shouldn't have to wear a muumuu because

you fill out a dress well," Cee said. "You should be able to wear the same dresses everyone else can."

Camille slapped the stone step. "It's not fair!"

"I've always loved my body," Stella said. "I'm curvy. I've got things other girls don't." She looked at me. "No offense."

I waved it off.

"But now," she continued with a hitch in her voice, "I feel humiliated. I kind of hate my body right now. It feels . . . wrong."

I reached out and placed my hand over Stella's. We weren't exactly best friends and she could be a snob sometimes, but I felt awful for her. This whole thing was ridiculous.

I squeezed her hand. "You are not *wrong*. You are beautiful. *They* are wrong."

Cee looked off into the distance, slightly shaking her head. "Between shutting down the Red Club and enforcing this ridiculous dress code, it seems like they're targeting girls."

Stella's expression darkened. "I'm no one's target."

Now *that* was the Stella I knew.

"Here's what we'll do," I said. "We walk up to the chaperone together, showing that we're wearing the same dress—"

"They won't let you back in," Camille interrupted. "Remember?"

"And I don't *want* to go in," Stella seethed.

"What do you want to do?" Cee asked.

Stella's green eyes flared. "I want to get revenge."

CHAPTER 17

I STOOD OUTSIDE THE GYM, NERVOUSLY wringing the strap of my backpack in my hand.

Cee strolled up with her own bag slung over her shoulder. Her crimson Harvard sweatshirt hung low over her black leggings.

"You can't wear leggings anymore," Camille said.

Stella snorted. "It's not a school day. And we're not going to be seen anyway."

"We hope," I muttered.

"Are you sure Janitor Mike isn't working today?" Cee asked.

Stella rolled her eyes. "Yes, I'm sure. It's Saturday, for one. And he worked late last night. He had to lock up after the dance committee did their cleaning."

Camille shifted her bag from one shoulder to the other. "If he locked up, how are we going to get in?"

Stella started walking and we fell in line, following her along the perimeter of the school. "Because I'm the head of the dance committee, and even though I wasn't allowed to *participate* in the dance, I was still allowed to clean up," she said bitterly. "And I left a way for us to get in."

She stopped by a metal door. I'd never been on this side of the school. It faced the woods, which I found creepy. I always went in and out of the main entrance or the side. I hadn't even known this back door to the gym existed.

Stella reached out and pulled the door open. A tiny stick had been lodged in the bottom corner, keeping it ajar. She held the door for me, but I hesitated. It wasn't like I'd never broken a rule before. I'd done a few shady things, but they'd been to get the story. Sometimes reporters had to break the rules for the greater good. This was different. This was revenge.

"Are you guys sure about this?" I asked.

"What's there to be sure about?" Camille said over

my shoulder. "It's a little prank. The boys pull pranks all the time."

Cee and I shared a look. I wondered if she was also having second thoughts.

Stella moved closer and got right up in my face. "They took away our Red Club. They took away our comfy clothes. They took away my special night at the dance. They took away your newspaper."

I felt my blood pressure rise as she ticked off each item.

Camille added, "And you've tried everything else. You tried getting an advisor. You appealed to Pickford. You asked who'd complained so you could reason with them."

"He wouldn't even publish your article on the dress code," Cee added bitterly. "They won't listen to us."

"But they listened to the complainer," Stella said. "Someone was unhappy, and they got so annoying about it that Pickford gave in."

"Maybe it's time that *we* got a little annoying," Camille said with a grin.

All the muscles in my face tightened. "Yeah, let's do this."

We filed in and put the stick back under the door for our quick way out. Enough sun came through the windows that we didn't need to turn on the lights. It was amazing that this was the same gym from the dance last night. There wasn't one cutout leaf or glitter star left. The dance committee had done a great job cleaning up.

But we were about to do some redecorating.

Stella dropped her backpack to the floor and unzipped it. "Did everyone bring their supplies?"

We nodded and muttered yes while we opened our bags and spread out our supplies. My heart pounded wildly in my chest, and I couldn't stop grinning. This was insane. But it was oh so fun.

The boxes were a rainbow of colors and brands, and inside were pads. As in the feminine-protection product. Giggling maniacally, we ripped the packages open and began to decorate. Each time I ripped the backing off a new pad and stuck it to the wall, a little thrill zipped through me.

We worked quickly, our little team of four, ripping and slapping until, finally, each pad had been placed. Breathing quickly, sweat dripping off our brows, we stepped back and examined our work. Maxi pads in all sizes and styles wallpapered the gym. Thin, overnight, with wings and without, scented and unscented. It was a cornucopia of pads.

"It's a masterpiece," Stella said.

"No." A smirk lifted the corner of Camille's mouth. "It's a menstrualpiece."

We doubled over laughing, that sort of over-tired, contagious gasping that happened late night at sleepovers. What we'd done was nuts, but it was also brave.

And I couldn't wait for the whole school to see it.

The whole school did not see it.

As soon as the first kid strolled through the gym Monday morning and spied our maxi masterpiece, they shut the place down. Gym classes were canceled for the morning, and Janitor Mike cleaned up our protest art.

I felt bad about that. I guess I hadn't thought through what would actually happen other than shock and (hopefully) discussion. I hadn't wanted to give Janitor Mike more work to do. He wasn't the one who'd shut down the Red Club.

But as the day progressed, something interesting started to happen. Word about the impromptu feminine art installation spread quickly. Everyone was talking about it. Whether with laughs and giggles or grossed-out shock, everyone knew.

It didn't take a genius detective to figure out that girls from the Red Club were the ones to wallpaper the gym in maxi pads. But it became more obvious when Stella bragged about it to a small group of her friends. And that small group whispered it to another small group, and soon enough all the kids knew who the four culprits were. And lots of girls had something to say to us.

"You should have invited me," one said while passing out papers in history.

"I would have loved to have helped," added another in the restroom.

"That was you guys, right?" a dozen whispered voices asked me throughout the day. "Awesome."

Even Cole found me at my locker. He leaned in close with a smirk on his face. "Nice decorating."

With all this attention, I expected Principal Pickford's voice to come booming out of the intercom at any moment, requesting my presence in his office. But it never came. I even passed by him in the hall and he only frowned at me and shook his head.

The only one who didn't want to talk about it was my best friend.

Ava tore off a piece of her turkey sandwich. "And then, after all that trash talk, she had a totally awkward landing. And I won."

I'd listened to the entire retelling of her weekend competition drama with an appropriate amount of nodding and smiling. I wanted to tell her all about the dance, what had happened to Stella, what we'd done to the gym. But she'd spent nearly the entire lunch period complaining about people I didn't even know and listing off her various muscle pains. She hadn't even asked about the dance.

"So enough about that," she said finally. "Important question."

I sat up straight in my chair, ready for her to ask if I danced with Cole.

"Are you ready for my party Wednesday?"

My shoulders sagged in disappointment.

"What?" she said, reading my body language. "You didn't forget, did you? You know this is important to me!"

I pushed my tray away. Even though I still had a few bites left, I wasn't hungry anymore. "I didn't forget. And yes, I'm still coming. But I thought you'd ask about something else."

She paused for a moment and her eyes flicked up to the ceiling like she was figuring out a math problem. Then she gasped. "Oh. Em. Gee. I am the worst friend in the world. I didn't ask about the dance! How was it?"

At the beginning of lunch, I'd been so excited to tell her every little detail. But now I didn't want to anymore. "It was fine."

"Did you dance with Cole?"

"Yeah."

Ava stared at me. "Yeah? That's it?"

I could have gone into detail—about how amazing it had been and how I'd felt like I could talk to him without getting nervous. But it was obvious that she didn't really care. I leaned back in my seat. "Do you still like gymnastics?"

"What?" Ava looked confused. "Of course. Why?"

"No offense, but you complain about it a lot. The other girls are mean to you. You're tired and sore. You have no time for anything else. You didn't even ask me about the dance until after you ranted about the competition." I stopped, hoping she wasn't mad at me.

Instead she took a deep breath and said, "Sometimes I hate it. Practicing every day isn't very fun. I'd rather just hang out and be normal. But at a comp, when I totally rock it and win?" Her eyes took on a dreamy look. "Then it's incredible. Those seconds when I'm soaring through the air and nailing a landing make the rest worth it. You can't have one without the other. I can't win without practice. So yeah, I still like it," she finished.

I guess I hadn't seen that look in her eyes in a while. I hadn't been to a competition of hers in a long time. But now I remembered. Yes, Ava at lunch could be whiny and complaining. But Ava at a comp was *fierce*. I admired that Ava. And I understood why she spent so much time on her sport, good days and bad.

The bell rang, signaling the end of lunch. Ava and I went our separate ways. But I only made it a few steps into the hall before Cee grabbed my arm.

She pulled me into an empty classroom, where Stella and Camille were already waiting.

"What's going on?" I asked, searching their faces.

"Something's happening," Cee said. "And I think it's going to help us get the Red Club back."

And just like that, I felt like Ava flying through the air off the vault, heart soaring.

CHAPTER 18

"DO YOU FEEL IT TODAY?" STELLA ASKED,
her green eyes twinkling.

We only had a few minutes before the next class
started, so I wished they'd get to the point of this secret
meeting. "Feel what?" I asked.

"The enthusiasm," Cee answered. "It's everywhere.
The girls really like what we did." She lowered her voice
at the last part, even though she wasn't really saying
anything incriminating like "maxi-padded the gym."

I leaned against a desk. "I did notice that. I've gotten a lot of questions. People wishing they'd helped us."

Stella beamed proudly. "We've awoken them. Shown them that it doesn't have to be the way it always was. There can be a new way."

"What do you mean?" I asked, still a bit confused.

Cee checked the hallway, then closed the classroom door. "This should be more than one prank. This should be a movement."

"The other girls will join us," Camille said.

A movement. I liked the sound of that. It sounded much more mature than "pranks." It sounded like something that could actually bring change.

"We could make people see things from our point of view," I said, getting excited. "Maybe we'd even get the Red Club back!"

I looked at the three of them, their eyes alight. Many girls had told me today that they wished they'd helped with our gym prank. But would they join a movement? There was only one way to find out.

"Okay," I said. "Let's have an emergency meeting. Send out a group text."

As Cee whipped out her phone, Stella added, "Tell them to share it with every girl they know who attended the Red Club. Even if for only one meeting."

"But where should we meet?" Camille asked. "Someone's house?"

I thought about what we'd said before. How the sixth graders could feel weird showing up at some eighth grader's house. "Too private. Starbucks?" I suggested.

Stella shook her head. "Too public. They'll be less likely to talk and share with a bunch of coffee drinkers listening in. What about the park? It's big enough that we can find a space just for us."

"At four o'clock the clubs and sports practices will be done," Camille added.

"That sounds good," Cee said. Her fingers flew over the letters on her phone. She added as many girls as she could to the text, hoping others would pass it on; then she hit send.

Now we just had to see if anyone showed up.

The park had an open field of grass and a playground with a slide, some swings, and a rickety climbing structure that I'd always been too chicken to attempt. But we were headed toward the gazebo. Which wasn't really a gazebo—that was just what we called it. It was much larger and more like a covered bandstand. The town had a concert every July Fourth, and the "gazebo" was the band's stage.

Today it was ours.

Or it would be, if anyone showed up. For now it was just the four of us. And a mother and child on the swings, but they seemed to be packing up and leaving.

Cee sat on the brown built-in bench. "So, who's going to run the meeting?"

"You," I said, as if it were obvious. "You ran the Red Club meetings this year."

"Yeah, but this is different. It's not just calling a meeting to order and seeing who has questions. We need, like, a motivational speaker." She motioned to Stella, who stood stiffly at the gazebo entrance, waiting for people to show. "Stella, you're the most fired up right now."

"But Riley is the best at convincing people," Stella said over her shoulder.

My mouth dropped open in surprise. Stella had never complimented me on anything before.

Stella rolled her eyes at my shock. "You know your articles are awesome. You have a way with words. You should run the meeting."

"We should all run it," I said. "Red Club doesn't belong to anyone. It's all of ours. We'll all speak. It'll just flow."

Camille snickered. "You said 'flow.'"

I sighed and looked out across the grass. No one yet and it was almost four o'clock.

There had been a ton of yeses on the group text, but that was different from doing the work. It was easy to say yes to a text. Much harder to leave the house and actually show up.

I swallowed hard as I started to wonder if no one would show. Maybe the Red Club didn't matter as much to other girls as it did to us. Maybe they didn't need the extra support and camaraderie. Maybe we were just *needy*.

No. I hadn't imagined the Red Club's effect on people. It meant something.

"You guys," Stella said, pointing toward the parking lot.

A group of girls poured out of the back of an SUV; then the mom sped away. Another group came in from the side, walking arm in arm. Then even more came, walking and jogging across the grass toward the gazebo.

Paige still had her cleats on from soccer. Julia, whose mom didn't even want her at *regular* Red Club meetings, pulled up with Hazel on bikes, faces flushed from pedaling the whole way.

They came right up to the gazebo entrance and

plopped down on the grass, as if expecting a performance. A feeling fluttered in my stomach. Not nerves . . . excitement. It was strange how I got nervous talking one-on-one with Cole, but here I was standing in front of twenty girls without a twinge of anxiety. The brain worked how it worked, I guess.

"Who's going to start?" Stella whispered.

I stepped out in front. "I will."

Gazing out at the sea of faces—from eighth-grade friends to barely familiar sixth graders—I was filled with hope. These girls had all come because they cared. Because they wanted change.

I cleared my throat. "I guess you all heard about the maxi-pad prank in the gym."

A chorus of giggles spread across the crowd.

"The ones who did it," I said carefully, "didn't do it for laughs. They didn't do it to cause someone clean-up work." I paused as I grasped for the right words. "They did it to tell people that they're fed up and they're not going to take it anymore."

The giggles stopped, and the girls sat up a little straighter and leaned forward.

I didn't really know where to go next, how to pull them all in. Maybe more of a conversation style would work, like the Red Club meetings.

I raised my voice. "Who here has felt ashamed when they have their period? Or scared that someone would find out?" I raised my own hand, and all the girls followed suit. "Someone tell me about that."

A sixth grader who'd gone to a couple of meetings, Prisha, spoke out. "I'm sick of working so hard to hide that I have my period. Like if a boy finds out I'm going to the bathroom to change my tampon, he'll think I'm gross or something."

"Yeah!" her friend yelled. "And it's not gross. It's normal."

Stella stepped forward. "Who has felt ashamed about their body? Boobs too big, boobs too small?" She raised her hand, as did everyone else.

Paige stood up and dusted some grass off her legs. "None of it makes any sense. You have to have, like, one percent body fat, but it all has to be concentrated in your boobs and butt."

A seventh grader from behind her added, "And you have to photoshop your pics for Insta. Filter your face. Change the shape of your waist."

Stella jutted her chin out. "We should all love ourselves. We shouldn't feel ashamed."

"I'm tired of hating myself for not looking perfect all the time," Julia complained.

Camille flipped her long hair over her shoulder. "People say they like the natural look, but the one day I didn't wear makeup, three people asked if I was sick."

Kristy nodded quickly. "I have to get up one hour earlier than my brother for school. Makeup, hair straightening . . . I spend all that time getting ready so I can look like someone else. Like not me."

"I love makeup, though," Stella said. "It's fun. If you're good at it—like me—it's basically an art form."

"You are awesome at makeup," I said. "And it's great that you love it. But I think Kristy's trying to say that she doesn't love it and feels pressured to wear it anyway."

"Huh," Stella said, like she'd never considered that before.

I followed the conversations back and forth, sometimes with a smile, sometimes with sadness, but always with support. And that was what it was all about. We had to get our Red Club back. It couldn't die forever. So many girls would need it in the coming years. We had to try.

Lin Cheung raised her hand. "So, what is this 'movement' you mentioned in the text? We're not just going to talk, right? What are we going to *do*?"

Stella's eyes twinkled. "We're going to cause a bit of a stir."

An excited buzz rose up from the crowd. I'd made the right move, opening things up for discussion first. It had pulled them all in, made it personal. And now we'd make our plan.

Cee clapped her hands to regain everyone's attention. "What would be *your* goals for the movement? Anyone?"

Julia raised her hand. "I want girls to be treated fairly."

Paige stood up. "I want to vent my anger. I want certain people to know that we're not going to take this anymore."

Stella clapped at that.

"I want my leggings back!" Vanita yelled, and a chorus of cheers followed.

"I just want the Red Club back," said a small voice from the back. I recognized her as a sixth grader who'd recently started coming to meetings.

Nods and words of agreement rose up from a bunch of others.

I cleared my throat. "And I'd like to make sure our plan doesn't cause innocent people any extra work."

Camille fake coughed into her hand. "Janitor Mike and the maxi pads, cough cough."

We spent the next half hour brainstorming ideas, working together, and coming up with our goals. Cee explained a concept from the world of psychology—she'd learned it from her psychologist dad—that would come in handy. Finally, our voices spent, we finished just as it started to get dark.

"Tomorrow is Tuesday," I said. "Everyone knows the plan?"

A murmur of agreement went through the crowd.

"And each day follows with its new objective," Cee said, "culminating in Friday . . . the reckoning. Remember to get other girls on board. Everyone has to participate Friday, or it won't work."

Excitement traveled through the group like electricity. We had the motivation, we had the desire, but I didn't know what would happen. Would it change anything at all?

It would be fun to find out.

Stella clapped her hands together. "Let the revenge of the Red Club commence!"

CHAPTER 19

TUESDAY MORNING, I STOOD OUTSIDE the main entrance to the school with an anxious feeling in my belly. It felt like waiting in line for a roller coaster. I was excited, I wanted to do this, but also . . . this might be very, very scary. Day one of the plan was here.

Part of me wanted to wait and see if the other girls were doing it. But what if they were waiting to see if others were doing it too? What if we were all waiting to see, and no one actually did it? Someone had to lead.

I slowly unzipped the small front pocket of my

backpack and reached my hand in for the thing. It was there. I had it in my fingers now. I just had to complete the task. I took a deep breath . . .

And pulled the tampon out.

I mean, it was still in the package and everything. I didn't pop it out of the applicator like a firecracker. But it would be totally clear to anyone looking that I was carrying a tampon. And that was the point.

Now or never, I told myself. Then I pushed open the front door.

Part of me wanted to slip by unnoticed, but that wasn't the point of the day. We were doing this to get attention for our cause. I hiked the backpack up higher on my shoulder, keeping the tampon in my right hand at all times. Each person I passed felt like a test. Would they notice? What would happen?

The first few people were too involved in their own stuff—grabbing a book from his locker, checking her phone, talking to a friend. But finally someone did notice. And it wasn't even a kid.

Miss Nancy, the principal's assistant, did a double take. Then she tilted her head to the side, like she was figuring something out, connecting the dots. But I breezed past, and she never said a word.

A hand clamped down on my shoulder.

"Oh, thank goodness you're here," Cee said as I turned around. She had a tampon in her hand too.

I held mine up. "Hey, same brand!"

"Are people noticing?" she asked, her eyes cutting left and right. "Has anyone said anything to you?"

I shook my head. "I just got here. Have you seen anyone else? Are they doing it?"

"Oh yeah. Stella is basically waving it above her head. A bunch of sixth graders walked down the hall twirling them like batons. Even some girls who weren't at the meeting."

"So, they're spreading the news like we asked," I said, pleased.

"Yeah. It's all happening. But that doesn't make me feel any more comfortable."

"Well, that's the point, right?" I reminded her. "To make people uncomfortable and then, eventually, comfortable. This was your idea."

"I know. It sounded great when I brought it up at the meeting. But it just feels weird. It's going to be a long, interesting day."

With that Cee headed off for her homeroom. I still had to make my way down the next hall to stop at my locker. I made it halfway there before an annoying voice yelled, "Oh, look! Riley's on the rag!"

I squared my shoulders and turned around to face Brody Scruggs. "What makes you say that?"

"Um, because of that lady stick you're not doing a great job of hiding in your hand." He snorted and elbowed his friend, who joined in with a fake laugh.

I held the tampon up in front of me like a Jedi wielding a light saber. "You mean this?" I waved it close to his face, right under his nose.

He stumbled back a bit. "Gross. What are you doing?"

I barked out a laugh. "What? Are you scared? It's not like it's used or anything. Though I could get you one of those."

His mouth dropped open. "You're disgusting." He turned on his heel to get away from me and ended up face-to-face with Julia, Stella, and Camille, who'd snuck up behind him, waiting.

"You have a problem with these?" Stella asked, and the three of them waved their tampons at his face.

Julia hissed, "You weren't scared of periods when you were calling me Bloody Julia."

His minion took off—smartly—but Brody was alone with us. And for the first time, I saw a glimpse of fear in the eyes of the bully who spent his time making others afraid.

"You girls are crazy," he said with a nervous twinge in his voice. "This is what happens when you're all on the rag at the same time."

Then he pushed his way between Julia and Camille and practically jogged down the hall.

Stella raised her eyebrows. "This is going to be a great day."

I aimed my thumb down the hall. "I have to get to my locker. See you guys later."

I finally made it, grabbing what I'd need for my first few classes. Then I closed the locker door and spun around to find Cole standing there. I'd been perfectly willing to embarrass myself for the cause in front of anyone else. But Cole?

His eyes drifted to my hand and the tampon, and his brow creased. "Can I ask you a weird question?"

"Um, sure."

His cheeks reddened slightly. "Do half the girls have their period at the same time or is this tampon thing the latest fashion accessory?"

A laugh escaped from me before I could hold it back. "Walk me to homeroom and I'll tell you what's going on."

He fell in step beside me. "So there *is* something going on. I'm not hallucinating!"

"You're not hallucinating," I said, laughing again. "Have you ever heard of exposure therapy?"

He gave me a funny look. "That is not how I was expecting this explanation to start. No, I haven't heard of that."

"Cee's dad is a psychologist," I explained, "so she came up with this idea based on something he does with his patients. He uses exposure therapy on clients when they're afraid of something they don't need to be afraid of."

"Like dogs?" Cole asked.

"Yes!" I exclaimed. "What Mr. Butler says is that when people avoid the things they fear, it makes their nervousness grow, because it's telling their brain it's right to be afraid."

"So rather than avoid dogs, they should be with dogs," Cole said.

"Yeah. First he'd make them hold a picture of a dog. Then be in the same room with a dog. Then eventually pet a dog. And after a while the brain makes new pathways or whatever and learns it isn't something to fear and the phobia usually goes away."

Cole stopped walking. "So are the girls carrying tampons around all day to make people face their fears with . . . period stuff?"

"Exactly! A girl shouldn't feel ashamed that people might see her bringing a tampon or a pad into the bathroom. So we figured if everyone is walking around all day carrying tampons, then people will get used to seeing them and it won't be such a big deal."

He paused for a long time. I hoped he didn't think the whole thing was totally stupid.

Finally he said, "That's brilliant."

A huge smile broke out across my face. "You think so?"

"Totally. It makes sense—the more you see something, the more normal it becomes."

"Exactly!"

"So, can I have one?" He held out his hand.

"Wh-what?" I stuttered.

"A tampon. Or pad. Or whatever. If the rest of the boys see that I'm not grossed out or freaked or whatever, that will help you, right?"

"Yeah, it really would," I said, surprised that he was brave enough to join in.

"Then . . . tampon me! Or whatever you ladies say."

I unzipped the front pocket of my backpack and pulled one out.

He took it in his hand and examined it for a moment. "I've never actually really looked at these before."

"They're pretty harmless," I said, laughing.

"To homeroom we go!" He held it up high, like a sword. "Hey, do you guys have anything else planned?"

"Oh, do we," I said with a grin. And I told him about our week.

The girls got looks all day from students and teachers alike. But the more people who carried tampons, the more others joined in. I was pretty sure I saw Ms. Bhatt carrying a tampon down the hall. And even Ava asked to carry one after lunch. Even better, no one got in trouble. I mean, how could they? A teacher wasn't going to check to see if you actually *had* your period or not.

A few more boys joined in after Cole took the lead. Some just because they thought it was funny, but many because they knew it was the right thing to do.

At the end of the school day, I leaned up against the wall near the front entrance, waiting for my bus. I felt someone sidle up next to me, and I expected to turn and see one of my friends. But it was Miss Nancy.

Her white hair was permed into tight curls, and she wore a pale blue dress that matched her eyes. I liked Miss Nancy. She always had a smile for the students and knew everyone's name. I'd hated seeing her walk through the cafeteria dress-coding girls. There had been a sadness on her face as she'd done it, like it was something she really didn't want to do.

"So," she said in my direction, "you seem to have tapped into some pent-up feelings among the girls."

"Me? What?" I pointed at my chest like I had no idea what she was talking about.

Miss Nancy just rolled her eyes, like *come on*.

A laugh bubbled up and out of me. But I didn't worry that she'd turn me into Principal Pickford or anything. And I hadn't really confessed, unless a laugh counted.

"Just be careful," she added. "You can't put the toothpaste back in the tube."

Confused, I asked. "What does that mean?"

"Nancy!" Principal Pickford's voice boomed from the office. "Where's Nancy?"

She pushed herself off the wall and gave me one last glance. "You set them free. They're not going to go back now."

I didn't understand her warning. That sounded fine to me. Freedom was the goal. I didn't *want* things to ever go back. It wasn't like the girls were going to go crazy and push things too far.

Stella and Camille danced past me and out the

double doors, having a sword fight with their tampons.

An eruption of laughter came from a crowd of boys as one of them—pretty impressively—juggled three super-absorption jumbos.

A group of sixth graders squealed and screamed as they dashed toward the bus, tossing a tampon back and forth in a game of hot potato.

Paige waved as she moved past me, holding a giant mobile made of tampons. "Check out the craft I made in art class!"

I swallowed hard. Yeah, this was fine.

My bus pulled up, and I grabbed the first available seat and stared out the window, collecting my thoughts. The theme of day one had been "no more hiding—tampons, tampons everywhere." I'd say it had been a huge success. Especially considering how nervous I'd been in the morning. But the girls had been totally brave.

That courage had to continue for day two's plan tomorrow.

CHAPTER 20

MY MORNING ROUTINE WAS PRETTY simple. I ran some anti-frizz serum through my hair to tame my waves. Then I put on a little bit of makeup—some mascara and eyeliner to make my eyes pop, and lip gloss to give my face some color. My mom had once told me I looked like a member of the undead without lip color, and while I thought that was a mild exaggeration, she did have a point. "Deathly pale" was my face's standard look.

Wednesday morning, I put no product in my hair. I didn't apply any makeup. And I chose a pair of old, baggy jeans and a big flannel shirt from the back of my closet.

I was ready much earlier than normal and strolled down the stairs, rather than my usual rushing in a blind panic because the bus was coming any second.

Mom looked up from her laptop at the kitchen table and gasped. "Are you okay? If you're not feeling well, you can stay home."

"I'm fine." I grabbed the cereal box from the table and filled a bowl.

Danny chewed through a spoonful, staring at me strangely. "Why are you wearing one of Dad's shirts?"

I looked down at the baggy flannel. "This isn't Dad's. I just don't usually wear it to school."

"Then why are you wearing it today?" Mom asked, trying her best to hide the judgment in her voice, but I heard it anyway.

"It's comfortable," I said, and shrugged. I really didn't want to get into the whole "I helped start a feminist movement at school" thing with her yet.

Dad came galloping into the room, singing at the top of his lungs. He was one of those weird people who woke up overflowing with happy energy. He stopped as he saw me and cast a quizzical look at Mom. She shook her head and mouthed something that looked like *moody teenager*, but I couldn't be sure.

Wednesday's theme was Natural Day. No hair straightening, no makeup, no transforming ourselves into other people. We come as we are. We love ourselves as we are.

Easier said than done.

On the bus, other girls sat low in their seats, their hoodies drawn up over their heads. Others had no idea what was going on because they were natural every day. And then there were the girls who hadn't participated—their flowing locks and flawless skin looking just as manufactured as ever. Those were the ones I narrowed my eyes at. A movement required total participation. But I was starting to learn that I couldn't count on everyone.

I nearly bumped right into Cee as soon as I walked through the main entrance. She had big, thick-rimmed glasses on. They were the pair she used to wear two years ago before she got contacts.

"I can't see a thing," she growled. "This prescription is old, and everything is blurry."

"It's only one day," I said. "You'll make it. And we'll make our point."

"Is it just me or is that wall moving?"

I took her by the elbow. "Let me walk you to homeroom."

We were almost there when an arm reached out from the girls' room and pulled me inside. I yelped, pulling Cee with me. Our kidnapper whirled around, shutting the door behind us and keeping it closed with her body.

"Hey!" a voice called. "Let me in!"

"Go away!" Stella screamed. "Find another one!" Her eyes flared with panic. Stella had always been the most confident of all of us, but right now she looked like she was on the verge of a breakdown.

"Hey," I said casually. "How's it going?"

"How's it going?" she repeated incredulously. "Look at me and tell me how it's going!"

I knew this day would be the hardest on Stella. Cee had an instinct for business, and I had a way with words. But Stella was the queen of makeup, hair, and fashion. And, for the day, that superskill had been stripped from her.

Cee squinted beneath her thick glasses. "Is that Stella?"

"Oh! Em! Gee!" Stella practically screamed. "My own friend doesn't even recognize me!"

"Cee's wearing her glasses with an old prescription," I explained. "She doesn't recognize anyone."

"I can't do this," Stella huffed, crossing her arms and beginning to pace. "I'm done. I don't have any problem with wearing makeup. I love it."

"And that's great," I said. "But remember the meeting, when some of the other girls who *don't* love it talked about feeling pressured to wear it? That's why Natural Day was voted on as one of the themes of the week. It's only one day. And it doesn't work if only some of us participate. We have to go all in. You said that, remember?"

Stella raked her hands through her tight red curls. "I know. I know you're right. But I look *really* different than I normally do. I don't want to be the person who's the *most* shocking. It's not that bad for you guys. Cee just tossed a pair of glasses on. And Riley's just dressing bad, which honestly isn't that unusual for her."

I pinched the bridge of my nose.

"I'm not going to make it through the day," she said.

"You will," I insisted. "You'll survive. And we'll have made our point. That we have to spend all this time transforming ourselves every day because of what society or the media dictates—"

My speech was interrupted as the door flew open.

Stella opened her mouth to yell at the restroom

intruder, but then she quickly snapped it closed. We all stood in our spots, silently staring.

Camille cocked her hip to the side and put one hand on it. "What are you staring at?"

Stella and I shared a look. We tried to share one with Cee, but she was leaning forward, squinting, in an attempt to figure out who'd joined us in the bathroom.

We were staring because Camille's trademark long, straight hair was the approximate size of Texas. It was as if someone with big hair got electrocuted and then went for a run on a day with 100 percent humidity. It was the biggest hair I'd ever seen. A photo of it belonged in the *Guinness Book of World Records*.

I realized that no one was answering, so I gently said, "Um, I didn't know you had curly hair."

"Or that much of it," Stella added.

Camille reached up and patted it, her hand momentarily disappearing and reappearing in the mass. "Isn't it gorgeous? The best part is that it's a choice. I can straighten it like I usually do or wear it big and curly like this. Lots of girls with straight hair could never do this. They're stuck with one style."

She flipped her hair around, grinning from ear to ear. And it *did* look awesome. At first it had been shocking because I'd never seen her wear it that way before. But the way she held herself and the way she flaunted it, Camille *rocked* that hair.

Stella, on the other hand, was feeling a different way. I could tell from the little smile on her face that she was pleased that she no longer had the biggest transformation. She turned to me. "Let's get to class. I'm not feeling all that self-conscious anymore."

Natural Day was progressing well for the most part, though Brody spent his morning shooting out insults like a T-shirt cannon at halftime. We gave him so much material to work with, he probably felt like he'd won the lottery. But I could tell that a few of his minions were tiring of their job. And one even gave me a secret thumbs-up behind Brody's back.

I chatted with Cole briefly in the hall, and he didn't even mention that my complexion was like a zombie's. So either he didn't notice, or he was too polite to ask. Either way, he got points. The person who didn't get points was my best friend.

First she gave me a weird look in math class. Then at lunch, she snapped, "Are we going to talk about this mess?"

"What?" I said through a mouthful of pizza.

She looked at me as if I'd grown a second head.

"You look like a slob, and it's the day of my party!"

Oh, that. Of course she only cared about her little get-together. I let out an exaggerated sigh. "It will take me two seconds to put some lip gloss on."

"And change your outfit to something super cute," she added.

"Would you like to come over and pick out my clothes, boss?" I snapped.

Ava's mouth opened slightly in surprise. I didn't usually talk back at her when she was in one of her bossy moods. I just ignored it or tried to put her in a better mood. But despite how much she thought the world revolved around this party, I had other things on my plate. Literally, like this slice of pizza that was about to bring me joy.

"What's up with you?" she asked.

"You could be a *little* bit interested in the Red Club movement," I reminded her.

She gasped. "I participated in the Tampon Challenge yesterday!"

"Only for the second half after everyone else was doing it. And you're not doing anything today."

She pointed at her face. "I can't do Natural Day. I never wear makeup anyway, and my hair is always up in a ponytail."

She had a point there, but I was still mad. "You could ask me how it's going. You could offer to do more. You were the one who was so upset last week when you got your period and the Red Club didn't exist to help you."

Ava chewed on her lower lip for a moment. "I'm sorry." Her voice trembled a bit. "I'm just so nervous about the party today."

"There's no reason to be nervous," I said, my anger starting to fade. "Everything will be fine."

She smiled. "And everything will be fine with your protest. Especially after the big day, Friday. They'll have to listen to your side."

"You'll do it too, right?" I asked her.

"On Friday? Of course! That's the most important day."

I took a big bite of my pizza, feeling better. Ava did care. She just sometimes forgot to show it.

"Do you want me to tell you all about the girls who are coming today, so you know what to expect?" she asked.

"Sure," I said through a mouthful. "Though I really hope I'm not expected to do any flips."

Ava giggled. "Just be your cool self. No flips involved."

CHAPTER 21

THE RED CLUB GIRLS WERE ALL GOING FOR ice cream at Dairy Queen before it closed for the season. That sounded much more appealing than hanging with girls I didn't know and listening to them talk about flips and stuff. But Ava needed me. And sometimes you had to do the right thing even if it wasn't your first choice. This was why I found myself walking across our front yards and up to her door for the party with her gymnastics squad instead of enjoying an Oreo Blizzard from DQ.

Lately, it felt weird to have this whole life separate from my best friend. It had been different when we were little. Living next door to Ava and without homework, clubs, and sports taking up our time, we were together constantly. We spent hours listening to music in her room and dancing. We'd gorge ourselves on candy while flipping through magazines, and talk and laugh until one of our parents told us to be quiet, which never worked.

People used to say we were "attached at the hip." But as soon as she started gymnastics, things started to change. And I knew we didn't have the same kind of connection now as we'd had before. I could feel it. But I didn't want to lose her completely. And I wanted to prove to her that I was a good friend and cared about what she cared about, even if I wasn't feeling the same thing from her.

As soon as the door swung open, Ava screeched and threw her arms around me like we hadn't seen in each other in weeks instead of hours.

"So glad you could come!" she gushed. "You look super cute. I love that top."

It was a top she'd bought me for my last birthday, so I'd figured it was a sure bet. But she was being so weirdly enthusiastic, it was kind of freaking me out.

She took my arm and led me into the living room,

where three girls were spread out across the sectional.

"Guys, this is my best friend, Riley," she announced. "Riles, this is Maylee, Maliyah, and Madilynn."

Riles? Who was Riles? She'd never called me that a day in my life. And Maylee, Maliyah, and Madilynn . . . really? How was I supposed to remember who was who?

The three *M*s all muttered some version of "hey," but they seemed super unimpressed. They were all tiny, like Ava, and wore their hair up in short pony-tails. They had identical glitter eyeshadow on, and one pulled Ava back down onto the couch and reached toward her with an applicator brush.

"We can do your eyes next," one of the *M*s said to me.

I shook my head. "That's okay. I'm good."

Ava shot me a look that I figured was disappoint-ment in my noncompliance. But I really had no inter-est in a communal glitter wand going anywhere near my eyeball.

I settled onto the nearest couch cushion. Awkward small talk came next, and I learned a little more about the girls. One was in seventh grade in the town next door. The other two were eighth graders at a local pri-vate school.

As the conversation steered toward gymnastics, I

mostly kept quiet and observed. The three *M*s seemed pretty tight-knit. Ava kept trying to insert herself into the conversation, but they often interrupted or spoke over her. I didn't know why she wanted so badly to impress these girls who didn't treat her all that great.

Mrs. Clement came around the corner carrying a silver tray full of cupcakes. The girls descended upon the treats as soon as she set the tray down on the table.

"Cheat day!" one screamed.

I plucked out a yellow cupcake with purple frosting, removed the liner, and took a bite. Mrs. Clement's cupcakes were always awesome. As were her cookies and basically anything else she made.

"Thank you, Mrs. Clement," I said through a mouthful.

She gave me a sad smile, like she felt guilty that I had to be there or something. "You're welcome, Riley."

One of the three musketeers cracked open a soda can and asked, "So what do you do?"

After a long awkward moment, I realized she was talking to me. I wiped a dab of frosting off my upper lip. "What do you mean?"

"Like a sport or something?" another *M* clarified.

Ava rearranged herself in between me and the *M*s. "Riley is our school's top investigative reporter."

"So, you write for the school paper," an *M* said, her eyes glossing over with boredom.

"She writes the most scandalous articles, you guys," Ava said, before I could get a word in about myself. "She gets in trouble all the time. Called into the principal's office and all that."

The bored *M* sat up a little straighter. "Really?"

"Yeah." Ava nodded quickly. "She pushed the limits so far that they shut the whole paper down two weeks ago."

"Whoa," all three *M*s said in unison.

That wasn't exactly true. But, I mean, Pickford was mad at me, and he had taken control of the paper, and he had put our publishing schedule on hold for a while. So, close enough?

Ava looked at me with an encouraging smile. She was pleased that the girls were interested. Might as well continue the tales of Riley.

I wiped the cupcake crumbs off my hands. "They also shut down my club because it was too inappropriate."

Six glittered eyes widened. "What kind of club?"

"It's called the Red Club. It's a period support group, but really, it's more than that. It's kind of like a sisterhood. And they took it away from us." I didn't even have to force the bitterness that tinged my voice.

Reaching for another cupcake, the closest M said, "You have to do something! You have to fight back!"

I grinned devilishly. "Oh, we are." And then I regaled them with tales of Tampon Day, Natural Day, and what we had planned for tomorrow.

The three Ms were a captive audience, asking questions now and then but mostly listening. They even high-fived me when I revealed our plans for Friday. Ava had sunk back into the couch cushions, not talking much, but I figured she had to be pleased with the turn her gathering had taken. The girls were happy and impressed. That was what she wanted, right?

"You should come to our next comp," an M said to me as she made her way to the door. The other Ms agreed. "Yeah, we want to hear everything about this week and how it went!"

"I'll definitely try to come," I promised. "Ava will get me the date and time."

"It was great to meet you!" they squealed, and offered up hugs before they ran down the driveway to their waiting cars.

Ava followed them outside, waving good-bye. I picked up some of the napkins and cupcake liners that littered the couch and floor since the other girls couldn't be bothered, I guess.

As I carried the garbage to the kitchen trash, the front door opened and slammed as Ava came back in.

"They were actually nicer than I thought," I said, wiping my hands on my jeans. "That went great, huh?"

Ava's cheeks were bright red. "Yeah, great. For *you*."

Completely confused, I shook my head. "What are you talking about?"

She pushed past me to get a drink from the fridge. "Thanks for totally stealing all the attention," she muttered.

"Stealing . . . attention . . ." I repeated the words slowly. "Wait, are you mad that they liked me? Wasn't that the point? You wanted me to impress them."

"*I* wanted to impress them!" she yelled, slamming her glass down on the countertop. "But it became the Riley show, and they only wanted to talk to you."

My mouth dropped open. I couldn't believe she was mad about this. "I was just making conversation. I thought you'd be happy. The girls were totally interested."

"Yeah, interested in *you*. I wanted this party to make them more interested in *me*. Your job was to make me look cool."

I clenched my jaw. "News flash, Ava. Everything isn't always about you!"

Ava gasped.

Now that I'd started, all the things I'd been holding in came tumbling out. "All you care about is the gym and your comps. You don't care about me or what's going on in my life."

"That's because you don't let me!" Ava screamed, her face red, her eyes filling with tears. "You keep me separate from Cee and your other friends. I wasn't allowed in your club. You're not the old Riley I used to be able to count on. I don't even know who you are anymore."

Her words hit me like a fist. This whole time I'd been upset that she wasn't like the old Ava, and she'd been thinking the same about me. Maybe we'd *both* changed.

I straightened my shoulders. "I'm *not* the old Riley. And you're not the old Ava. We're not the old us. So we should stop trying to pretend that we are."

Then I turned and left my best friend's house, wondering if it would be for the last time.

CHAPTER 22

THURSDAY WAS SUPPOSED TO BE THE FUN
day. The theme was "Say it loud, say it proud; the
secrets of girlhood are no longer secret." Basically, we
would say the words we usually kept to ourselves or
whispered. I'd been looking forward to it ever since we
made the plan. But now I could barely drag myself to
my locker.

After Ava's party, I'd gone to bed without dinner,
claiming a headache. Though it wasn't a lie. I did have
a headache . . . and a stomachache . . . and a heartache.

The girls were practically giddy in the halls, loudly

saying the "inappropriate" things we usually only whispered about.

"Aunt Flo is in the house!" Lin yelled as she strolled by with two friends.

"With her Cousin Red!" called her friend.

The last of the threesome shouted, "My uterus is shedding its lining!"

Lin and the middle girl stopped and stared, "We're using *metaphors*, Miranda."

I didn't even laugh. I shrugged off the zip-up hoodie that I used as a fall jacket and hung it in my locker, then pulled out my books. I'd been looking forward to this day. We were all going to talk about our periods, whether we currently had them or not, as loudly as possible. It would drive trolls like Brody crazy. And it would feel good. But instead I felt terrible.

Stella and Camille came up on either side of me as I slogged toward homeroom.

"Ugh, I have cramps," Stella said in an obviously exaggerated yell.

Camille reached over my head to high-five her. "We're blood sisters!"

Stella slapped her hand, neither one of them realizing yet that I wasn't really into it. "I'm day one," Stella shouted. "Flood day."

Camille grimaced. "Ugh, that's rough. I'm day five. Panty-liner day."

Cee strolled up to make us four across. "Weird, my heaviest is day two, not one. And I don't get to wear a liner until day seven."

"Seven?" Camille put a hand over her heart. "Oh my goodness!"

"Mine's only four days total," Stella said.

"So jealous!" Cee said, her eyes cutting to me, as if wondering why I wasn't playing along.

Ms. Bhatt and Mrs. Hopkins had walked out of the teachers' lounge together, right in the midst of the loudest menstrual cycle–tracking conversation in Hawking Middle School history.

Mrs. Hopkins bristled. "Girls, please. Can we behave like ladies?"

"We *are*," Stella said. "Ladies have periods."

Mrs. Hopkins shook her head and moved on, but Ms. Bhatt smirked.

Stella and Camille giggled and ran off, prattling on about jumbo tampons.

Cee nudged me with her elbow. "What's up? You're not embarrassed, are you?"

"Not at all. I was looking forward to this."

"Then . . ."

I heaved a sigh. "I had a huge fight with Ava yesterday. I said terrible things. She said terrible things. And I feel awful."

"I think the feeling is mutual." Cee motioned with her chin.

I turned to see Ava staring at me from a classroom doorway. She looked miserable, maybe even worse than me. Once I noticed her, she hung her head and turned away.

The warning bell rang.

"Gotta go!" Cee called.

I got through homeroom and my first class and then forced myself to forget about Ava for the time being and focus on the day's mission. I even got into a healthy debate about menstrual cups—period innovation or abomination?—in the hall on the way to my second class.

The theme of the day seemed to be working *really* well. So many girls were participating. The problem was that, as the day went on, the girls liked it a little too much. Rather than keeping it in the halls as planned, they brought it into the classrooms. They interrupted the teachers. Miss Nancy's weird warning about toothpaste echoed in my head as I walked into the cafeteria for lunch. But then a brand-new worry spiked in my brain.

Cee, Stella, and Camille had second lunch. It was always just Ava and me together at first lunch. But what would I do now? I peeked around the open doorway and saw that Ava wasn't seated yet. Maybe she'd skip lunch or eat somewhere else and I wouldn't have to deal with it. We didn't walk together out of math class, so she could be anywhere.

I got in line and chose a slice of cheese pizza and a side salad. But when I finished at the register and turned back around, I froze in place. Ava was now in her regular seat like she was waiting for me. The sight of her sitting there with her sad-looking sandwich and even sadder eyes made my heart hurt. But I wasn't ready to make up or even talk to her. Not yet.

But if I didn't grab my regular seat, where else would I go? I gripped the tray tightly in my suddenly sweaty hands and scanned the cafeteria. At Hawking Middle School everyone had their place. It wasn't so much cliques like jocks and nerds, band geeks and wannabes. It was groups of tight friends. And I didn't see any room for me.

"Hey, are you okay?" a soft voice came up from behind me.

I glanced over my shoulder and saw Julia exiting the line with her own tray. "Um, yeah, I just . . . um.

My friend and I, uh." There was no way Julia was going to understand my incoherent babbling.

Julia's eyes went to Ava sitting alone and then back to me standing frozen in place. "Would you like to sit with me and Hazel today?"

I breathed out a huge sigh of relief. "Yes, thanks."

"It's not a problem. Someone once did a favor for me with a quick sweatshirt move in math class. Figured I'd pay it forward." She grinned, and I managed a weak smile back.

I settled in at the new table. Julia and Hazel talked about their favorite TV show, which I'd never watched or even heard of, but I laughed and nodded in the right parts.

Lunch was halfway over when someone yelled, "I'm on the rag!"

I paused with my pizza slice in midair, and half the cheese slipped off and fell to the tray.

"What was that?" Julia asked.

"I got my red wings!"

I turned in my seat and saw two girls—both sixth graders—on opposite ends of the cafeteria, standing up on the tables. What in the world was going on? This was *not* part of the plan.

A third girl, closer to us, scrambled up to standing

on the table, knocking over milk cartons along the way. She cupped her hands around her mouth and yelled, "The tomato soup is on the boil!"

The shocked silence of the lunchroom immediately turned to laughter. Kids couldn't believe it. One girl after the other stood and yelled some period metaphor.

"I'm riding the cotton pony!"

"The painters came to town!"

"It's time for the great flood!"

"I have the red badge of courage!"

"Was this supposed to happen?" Julia asked me, raising her voice to be heard over the hysterical laughter. "Yelling period metaphors at lunch?"

I shook my head, panic rising in my throat. "No. This must have grown on its own."

"I got the girl flu!"

"It's flooding down south!"

The lone lunch monitor, a first-year teacher named Mr. Wixted—who was about twenty-two and looked completely horrified—held up his hands. "Girls, please! That's enough!"

But they didn't listen. More and more stood up.

"I'm howling at the red moon!"

"I've opened the floodgates!"

Mr. Wixted ran out of the room and came back moments later with Miss Nancy. The lunchroom had descended into chaos.

A few kids started to throw food. Kids were screaming.

No, no, no. This was getting totally out of control.

Miss Nancy's eyes widened as she took in the situation. And then, somehow, they found mine. I made a small shake of my head as if to say this wasn't what I'd wanted. This wasn't me. But she'd warned me, hadn't she? I'd started this, and now it had taken on a life of its own. We'd lost control.

The lights in the cafeteria flickered off and on, catching everyone's attention, and we turned to see Principal Pickford standing in the doorway, his hand on the light switch, his face twisted into red-cheeked fury.

"Lunch is over!" he hollered, his booming voice echoing off the walls. "I don't care if you're not finished. Grab your things and wait outside your next classroom."

I tossed my half-eaten pizza and untouched salad and dashed out, head down, trying my best not to make eye contact with anyone from administration. Classes started as normal. But halfway through the next period, all teachers were interrupted by the intercom.

"Please excuse the interruption for this important message," Mr. Pickford said, his voice deep and controlled. "There will be no more distractions like there have been this week. No excuses. We are in full crackdown mode and will be levying punishments on anyone seen or *heard* disrupting any part of the school day—including lunch and between classes. These punishments will include suspension."

Light gasps came from a few girls in class. My heart pounded wildly in my chest. Tomorrow was Friday, the most important day. We needed unity, a show of strength, or it wouldn't work. But now, with the threat of punishment hanging over our heads, would everyone still band together?

CHAPTER 23

I STOOD AT THE ENTRANCE OF SCHOOL
on Friday morning. The day of reckoning. The day the
girls would stand together in the face of unfairness. Or
sit in class. Or walk in the hall. Whatever. All that mattered was that we banded together. And by that I mean
wore leggings.

Cee, Stella, Camille, and I had spent the night
before debating in group text. Did we really want to fla-
grantly break the rules the morning after Mr. Pickford
had threatened suspension? It was a risk. But one we'd
decided we had to take. We'd started this movement

to protest unfairness toward girls in school, and if we stopped now, we'd accomplish nothing. Friday was the big day it had all been leading up to. The movement had started small, with the Red Club girls, but had grown over the week with more and more kids participating. Today was meant to be our biggest protest yet. And it required no words, no embarrassment, just a simple clothing choice.

Cee came up behind me and rested her chin on my shoulder. "What do you think? Will it work?"

"It has to," I said in an almost whisper.

"Are you nervous?"

I glanced down at my long, flowy purple shirt and the black leggings I wore underneath. Prohibited, evil, demon leggings. "Yep."

She looped her arm through mine as we headed toward the main entrance. "Don't worry. We're all going to be wearing leggings. They can't suspend everyone."

I took a deep breath and straightened my shoulders. I put my hands on my hips. A power stance. I was ready. After all, well-behaved women rarely made history.

I gripped Cee's arm. "Let's do this."

But as soon as we passed through the double doors

of the entrance, everything was wrong. Girls in leggings were already sitting on the floor of the hallway, lined up outside the office. And, even worse, everyone else seemed to *not* be wearing leggings. My eyes darted around the hall, taking in girls' outfits—jeans, khakis, skirts—the vast majority were not following the plan. And when they noticed me and Cee, they cast their eyes down and hurried away.

"You!" a voice boomed out. "And you."

Cringing, Cee and I turned to face Principal Pickford and his giant pointing finger.

"Get in line with the others," he said. "Your parents will be called to come get you."

Cee and I joined the short line of girls in leggings and slumped down the wall to the floor. Camille and Stella soon joined us.

"Well, at least we're comfortable while we're waiting for our execution," Camille said.

Stella glared at a sixth grader in khakis as she slunk past. "I can't believe most of the girls chickened out."

I sighed and put my head down on my knees.

"This is so unfair," a deep voice said.

Cee gave me a sharp elbow, and my eyes snapped open. I found myself staring at two high-top sneakers. My eyes roamed up a too-short, ill-fitting pair of leggings . . . and found Cole standing before me.

I scrambled up to standing, though I still had to look up because the kid was so darn tall. "Yeah, totally unfair," I said.

Cole shook his head in disgust. "Like, what's more distracting in class . . . a girl dressed comfortably in her seat or a kid like Brody talking and throwing pencil erasers the whole time?"

"I KNOW, RIGHT?" Camille shouted from the floor.

I shot her a look, and she made a *zippering it shut* motion across her mouth.

I turned back to Cole. "I can't believe you wore them."

He grinned sheepishly. "I got a whole bunch of my friends to do it too."

Then a whole bunch of his friends are getting suspended, I thought. *And it's my fault for telling him the plan.*

"No," he said, pointing at me. "Don't feel guilty. We decided this on our own."

"And they weren't the only ones," Camille said, laughing.

Several members of the football team walked past, with Mr. Pickford yelling at them to line up against the other wall.

The quarterback, Warner Washington, nodded his head at me.

"*You're* wearing leggings?" I said in shock.

He shrugged. "It seemed like the right thing to do. I don't see the difference between leggings and football pants, but no one would blink an eye if I wore my uniform to school on game day."

"Well, thanks," I said.

He nodded again and went over to join his teammates.

I couldn't believe the number of people who didn't participate in Leggings Day, but I also couldn't believe the people who did. I even spied Ava sitting at the far end of the line of girls. We locked eyes for a moment. I was proud of her for joining in. But would any of it matter?

The bell rang shrilly, echoing through the hall. I felt that instinct to rush to class, but I couldn't. I was stuck here waiting for my parents to get called. I'd miss out on so much, maybe even a pop quiz.

Cole's leggings-wearing friends called out, waving him over to the opposite wall.

"You'd better join them while you can before your parents ground you," I said.

He leaned forward and whispered, "I'll just blame

this girl I like. She's kind of a bad influence." Then he winked and ran off.

My jaw dropped open, but I quickly shut it because it felt like my heart was going to soar right up my throat and out of my body. I turned to the other girls to see if they'd heard, but they were whispering among themselves, comparing notes about what they thought their punishments would be. And that brought me right back down to the floor—literally.

"I really thought today would work," Cee said. "That they'd realize the only education that was getting interrupted was ours. That they'd see us all together and realize they couldn't send us all home."

But only twenty girls wore leggings. And twelve boys. And, yes, they sent us all home.

My mother didn't speak to me during the car ride. Not one word. In a way, that was even worse than getting yelled at. Mr. Pickford had decided to "go easy on us" and just send us home for the day—no suspensions. But on Monday each student, with a parent, had to meet with him in his office. So I had that to look forward to over the weekend.

When we got home, Mom pointed at the staircase and said, "To your room. I'll call you down for dinner." That was it.

I overheard her on her cell canceling her house-showing appointments for the day. What did she think? That she had to work from home to keep an eye on her delinquent daughter?

Once the school day ended for everyone else, the texts started rolling in. The excuses were varied.

I forgot it was today.

My mom wouldn't let me.

All my leggings were in the laundry.

But I knew the truth. They'd been scared to get in trouble. And could I blame them? Most girls weren't as familiar with Principal Pickford's office as I was. They feared that label. *Trouble. Bad girl.* So while I was disappointed that we hadn't taken this giant, unified stand, I shouldn't have been surprised.

And now what would happen? We had no further plan.

I buried myself under the covers of my bed and called Cee.

"So, what's your punishment?" she asked instead of saying hello.

I picked at a piece of lint on my purple bedspread. "I don't know yet. Mom won't even talk to me. I'm terrified for dinnertime."

"Oh yeah." Cee giggled. "The Dunne Family Dinner Game is going to be extra interesting tonight."

I raked a hand down my face and groaned. "How about you?"

"My parents are fine with it. They're proud of me for taking a stand."

Of course they were. Cee's parents were cool. Meanwhile, my mom was probably drawing up a written contract for my long-term grounding, and my dad would just go along with whatever she decided.

"So, what do we do now?" Cee asked. "What's the Red Club's next step?"

I'd been thinking about that myself, and I hadn't come up with a good answer. "I don't know. Nothing's working. Pickford isn't changing his mind."

"I'm not ready to give up, though," Cee said.

"Me either, but I don't know where to go from here. If we keep pulling the same stunts, we'll just keep getting in trouble."

"But there has to be something else we can do."

I thought about where this had all begun: with that school committee meeting and the mysterious complaints. "I wish I'd figured out who the secret complainer was. Even though your mom said it wouldn't make much difference, I just want to know who got our club shut down."

"If you're not grounded, maybe we can meet at my house tomorrow," Cee suggested. "Go over your list of suspects. See if there's anything you missed. Tell your parents it's for a project."

Not a lie. This *was* a project.

"Riley!" Mom's sharp voice echoed from downstairs. "Dinner!"

"Yikes, even I heard that," Cee said. "That's her angry voice."

I closed my eyes and took a deep breath. "Pray for me."

"I will. You'll need it."

CHAPTER 24

I PADDED DOWN THE STAIRS AS QUIETLY as possible and slipped into my seat at the table, wishing I were invisible.

Danny looked at me, his brow furrowed in confusion. *Why is Mom acting weird?* he mouthed.

I shook my head quickly. Maybe if it didn't get brought up, I wouldn't be murdered right there at the dinner table. But Danny crossed his arms and pouted at my silence. He hated being left out of drama.

Even Dad entered the room as quiet as a cat and looking just as skittish. I stared at him, hoping for some sort of sign to see whose side he was on. But he just stared down at his empty plate.

Wait . . . Mom had cooked last night. They usually alternated. This made no sense.

"Why is Mom cooking?" I whispered to him. "It's your night."

He glanced at me quickly. "She said she wanted to. She needed to . . . keep busy."

Wow. Mom was so mad that she chose to cook on her night off. Either that or she was purposefully poisoning my food.

"Just tell me," I said in a hushed voice. "Am I about to be murdered at the dinner table?"

Dad rolled his eyes. "Stop."

Danny perked up. "What did you do?" He rubbed his little hands together. "This is going to be good."

Mom strolled in holding a platter of meat loaf and placed it in the middle of the table. It looked innocent enough, but I waited for someone else to take a bite first. Okay, no poison.

"So," Mom said, suddenly breaking the quiet. "Time for the game."

My fork fell into a mountain of mashed potatoes. For real? Cee had only been joking. We weren't *really* going to play this game tonight.

As if she could read my mind, my mother said, "Tradition is tradition, and we're not going to skip a night because of *someone's* day."

That someone being me.

Danny piped up. "I'll go first! A good thing about today was that James said I wasn't any good at kickball but then during recess I was up and kicked the ball right into his face. And the thing I'm looking forward to is finding out what Riley did so wrong that Mom is going to murder her at the dinner table."

Mom's eyes shot daggers at me over a bowl of green beans.

Dad coughed into his hand. "Okay, I'll go next. A good thing about today was that I closed a deal I'd been working on for a couple weeks. And the thing I'm looking forward to is this dinner being over."

Everyone looked at me next. But I couldn't take my turn. All these feelings were twisting and turning inside me like emotion soup. I felt like if I started talking, I'd burst into tears.

Mom dabbed at the corner of her mouth with a napkin and said, "Fine. I'll go. My favorite part of the day was getting a call from the school to come pick up my rule-breaking daughter. And the thing I'm looking forward to is our appointment with the principal on Monday. Just what a mother dreams of."

I gripped my fork tighter. "You're acting like I set a house on fire."

"You got sent home from school."

"For wearing comfortable clothes!" I snapped. "The horror! Lock me up now! Reserve my room at the local juvenile prison!"

"Riley," Dad warned.

But I couldn't stop. The floodgates were opened. The lump that had been sitting in my throat had dislodged, and I'd found my voice.

"I'll take my turn." I put down my fork and clasped my hands together like a little lady. "My favorite part of the day was when I led a movement against unfair, sexist rules and my own family wasn't supportive of me."

"A movement?" Mom repeated. "You're the ringleader of a group of troublemakers."

I shook my head fervently. "Not troublemakers. Girls who want fairness. Girls who have been made to feel ashamed and humiliated. Girls who've never used their voice but are sick of being quiet."

Dad got up from his chair and tapped Danny on the shoulder. "Let's go. Mom and Riley need to talk."

"But I'm not finished eating," he whined. "I'm still hungry."

"We'll go out for ice cream," Dad promised, pulling him up out of his seat.

"But this was just getting good!" Danny's voice echoed on his way out of the room.

I brought my eyes back to my mother's. "I have to finish my turn. The thing I'm looking forward to is someday, somehow, finally making my mom proud."

She blinked quickly. "Stop that nonsense. You know I'm proud of you."

"You're not." My voice trembled. "You wish I was a quiet little girl who only cared about pleasing people and not causing a stir. All you want is for me to be a ladylike, nice girl. But I want to be me. I want to raise my voice and stand up for myself. And stand up for others. I don't want to be quiet. I don't want to have to hold all my feelings inside."

Mom got up and came around the table to sit in the chair beside me. Her expression softened. "You really feel like that? Come on. You know I love you."

I swallowed hard, holding back tears. "Yes, you love me, but you kind of *have* to. I think you wish I was different, though. Another type of girl."

Her mouth opened and closed, and she hesitated before speaking. "I don't wish that. I'm just . . ." She looked away and stared at the wall for a long time. So long that I thought she'd fallen asleep with her eyes open. What could she possibly be thinking about this whole time?

Finally she spoke again. "You know how I grew up. You know how Grandma is."

Oh boy, did I know. Mom had told me stories about growing up with Grandma and her strict rules. Mom wasn't even allowed to wear pants! Just dresses, all the time, to look "like a lady." And I was sure there was more that Mom hadn't yet told me. But still . . .

"Just because Grandma is a certain way, that doesn't mean you have to repeat—" I stopped myself from saying *her mistakes*. I didn't want to make Mom feel bad. She already looked like she wanted to cry.

She let out a sigh that sounded like it had been held in for a year. "I know we don't have to all be our mothers. I can see that in what a free, outspoken young woman you have become. You're nothing like me." There was a sad twinge in her voice. "It's hard for people to change, if they grew up a certain way or find themselves stuck in their ways."

I didn't know what to say. We'd never really talked like this before.

Mom pushed a strand of hair away from my eyes and cupped my face in her hands. "But that doesn't mean they can't try to change," she said, her eyes welling up. "I'm sorry if I've made you feel like you can't share your feelings."

That lump returned to my throat, and this time it was the size of a baseball. "Okay."

She leaned forward and rested her chin on her hand, examining my face in that Mom way. "How *are* you feeling?" she asked. "And be honest."

I exhaled loudly. "I'm angry. I'm tired. And I'm tired of being angry."

"Well, that's okay."

I gave her a look. "It is?"

"It's all right to be angry. What matters is what you decide to *do* with that strong emotion."

Like not get sent home from school was what she meant. And I understood that. All the stuff I'd done at school had only served to distract. It hadn't solved anything.

I chewed on my lower lip. "I don't know what to do anymore. I feel like I put in all this effort and we're right back to where we started. We accomplished nothing."

"It sounds like you're ready to give up. That's not the Riley I know."

"I don't know what else I *can* do. We did all this work, and we didn't create any change."

"Do what you do best. Use your superskill."

I didn't see the point. I'd already tried that. Mr. Pickford wouldn't publish it. I didn't even know if he'd bother to read the next article before he tossed it in the trash. I sighed. "But the newspaper—"

Mom cut in. "Who said it had to be for the paper? Remember when you got that idea for a blog?"

"And you said I didn't have the time," I reminded her.

Mom reached out and grabbed my hand. "Maybe now's the time after all."

I paused for a long moment. "Do you really think people would read it?"

"I know a few girls who definitely would. And then they'd share it on their phones like you all do. It would get around the school."

"Thanks," I said.

She leaned back in her chair. "Now, about your punishment."

I winced, waiting for the details of the Grounding to End All Groundings.

"You do the dishes every night for a week."

I opened my eyes and let out a breath. That couldn't be it. "And?"

Mom gave me a small smile. "And you have to spend some time with me this weekend, telling me all the stuff you've been holding back—about these unfair rules, this Red Club movement, everything. I want to be armed with information when we go to meet with the principal on Monday."

I nodded quickly, tears threatening to appear in the corners of my eyes again. "I can do that."

"Okay." She patted my leg. "Go clean up."

I went into the kitchen and started on the dishes with a big smile on my face. Sure, it was great that my punishment wasn't severe. But more important, this was the first time in a long time that I felt like Mom and I had really connected. And it felt wonderful.

As I was finishing up, Danny skipped into the room with a chocolate ice cream mustache. "I got ice cream and you didn't," he teased in a singsong voice.

But it didn't even annoy me. "Oh well," I said, and ruffled his already-messy hair.

And then, because my day hadn't been strange enough, he threw his little arms around my waist and said, "I'm glad you didn't get murdered at the dinner table."

"Thanks, buddy," I said, holding back a laugh. "Me too."

CHAPTER 25

WHEN CEE INVITED ME OVER SATURDAY to discuss my investigation into who'd complained about the Red Club, I didn't expect it to be so organized. Though I should have. I mean, it was Cee.

"Since when do you have a whiteboard? And why?" I asked as she placed a marker into my hand.

"It helps me to work out business problems when I write them up on the board. Or even pro-and-con lists. New ideas. I use it all the time. It was a great investment."

"Let me guess. You bought it at a garage sale."

"Five bucks!" She beamed. "From a retired teacher."

Cee wanted me to write all the suspects up on the board so we could gather evidence, but the truth was, I hadn't had time to think about too much. I'd spent all night writing my article and all morning filling my mom in on every detail like she'd asked. Then she'd gone into her own office to do "research." She allowed me to go to Cee's house while they went to Danny's soccer game. And now I was promptly put on the spot.

"C'mon, Ms. Investigative Reporter, let's do this." Cee nudged me forward.

I uncapped the marker and took a deep breath. "Well, we have the obvious." I wrote *Brody Scruggs* on the board.

Cee nodded. "Brody hates us, that's for sure."

"And I may or may not have tripped him after a Red Club meeting when he bullied Julia," I admitted.

Cee smirked. "But I can't picture him booking time with Principal Pickford to complain about the Red Club. He wouldn't be able to put forth a coherent argument."

True. But his mother could. "Mrs. Scruggs complained about the dress code at the school committee meeting. She went on and on, blaming girls in leggings for Brody's bad grades."

Cee groaned in frustration. "Totally the type of mom who would go to the administration to get a girls' club shut down. Especially one that her precious baby doesn't like." She rubbed her chin for a moment, staring at the board. "Okay, who's next?"

I thought for a moment. "Julia's mom."

"You still think she could have done it?" Cee asked. "She wasn't at the school committee meeting."

"But she could have complained to Pickford privately. Julia told me that her mom didn't approve of the Red Club."

Cee's eyes narrowed. "I'll never understand people who want to make rules for all children rather than their own kid. If she didn't want Julia to go to meetings, fine. But would she really try to make it so that all girls couldn't go?"

I shrugged. "I don't know." The Alperts were new in town. I'd never even met Julia's mom, so I had no idea what kind of person she was.

"Put her on the list," Cee said.

I did, the marker squeaking as I wrote. "I wish there was a way to find out more about her, to get a sense of her."

Cee tapped a pink painted fingernail on her chin. "We could do some light Facebook stalking."

I did a double take. Cee was old enough for an account, but no one in our grade had one. It was more for grown-ups. "You have a Facebook account?"

Cee shrugged. "It's how I get notifications from my local Future Business Leaders of America chapter."

But of course.

"My stuff is charging downstairs," she said. "Can I log in on your laptop?"

"Sure." I walked over to her glass-top desk and opened the computer I'd brought. My most recent document—the article I'd been working on—was up on the screen. I opened a browser window for Facebook.

Cee dragged over a second chair she had in the corner and pushed me over a bit to share the space. She logged in quickly and her feed loaded. As expected, it was all business and self-motivation pages.

"Let's see if Mrs. Alpert has an account."

I wouldn't even have known where to start looking, but Cee immediately clicked to a Hawking Middle School group and opened up the list of its members.

"Ah. Susie Alpert. Here she is." Cee pointed at a small square photo next to the name. The woman looked just like Julia, only older and with a mom haircut.

Cee clicked to Mrs. Alpert's page and we looked around, but there wasn't much to see.

"Why is it mostly blank?" I asked.

"She's using her privacy settings." Cee sighed. "Good for her, but bad for us stalkers."

Cee shut down the browser, and my article filled the screen. She leaned forward in her chair. "What's this?"

"Oh, that's . . ." *What I worked on all last night, staying up way later than usual, pouring my heart and soul into.* "Just an article."

"For the paper? I thought Pickford wasn't having meetings right now and you guys were on hold."

"We are," I said, "and even if we weren't, he definitely wouldn't publish this. But I felt like I had to write it anyway, to get it all off my chest and onto paper. Or . . . laptop. I thought maybe I could publish it myself on a blog, but I don't have a blog and I wouldn't even know where to start."

"Can I read it?"

"Sure." I moved aside to give her the full view of the screen.

She read slowly and quietly, chewing on her thumbnail the whole time. Now and then I noticed her giving a slight nod. When she was done, she pushed the laptop away and gazed up at me.

"Wh-what did you think?" I asked, suddenly nervous.

"I think that's the best piece you've ever written. And I think that we're setting up that blog, right now."

My heart sped up. "You'll help me?"

She poked a finger at the screen. "Everyone in school needs to read this. If I have to share the blog post with every girl, boy, and teacher myself, I'll do it."

I threw my arms around her neck. "Thank you, you Internet wonder!"

"And while I create the account, choose a template, and design a header, you work on the investigation."

"Okay." I nodded, even though I only understood a little bit of what she'd said.

Cee started clicking away at the keys on my laptop, and I leaned back in the chair and tried to refocus on the investigation. I wrote a few more names on the board, including my mother's, but then I stopped. Mom thought the Red Club was inappropriate. She didn't like that I was a part of it. But we'd shared a lot over the last day. We'd gotten so much closer. I wasn't sure about a lot of things, but I was sure about this one.

I crossed her name off the list.

My mom wasn't the secret complainer. I was sure of that now. But that didn't help me figure out who was.

CHAPTER 26

BY MONDAY MORNING, MY BLOG WAS UP and running. Stella and Camille had texted me to say that the post was "amazing," and they were going to share it all over school and on social media. Even my parents read and loved it. I think it made them understand me a bit more. But none of that mattered if Principal Pickford wouldn't see it and pause to really *think* about what I wrote.

As I walked through the main doors of school, I got that chased-by-a-bear feeling again. My heart was pounding; my breath came too fast. I'd been in Principal

Pickford's office before, but never with my mother. It had always been for little things that I could easily talk my way out of. I wouldn't be able to talk my way out of this.

Mom pushed open the door to the main office and approached the desk. It was early. The first bell hadn't even rung yet. I stood beside her, wiping my sweaty hands on my jeans. I wished my dad were with us too. He could crack one of his corny jokes and lighten the mood. But he'd said he had a meeting he couldn't miss and that I shouldn't worry because "Mom has this." Whatever that meant.

I coughed into my hand. "Um, excuse me, Miss Nancy. We have an appointment with Principal Pickford."

Miss Nancy looked at us over the rim of her glasses. "You're next? I could have sworn it was someone else. We're very busy here this morning."

Due to Legging-palooza, which was my fault. I felt my cheeks turn red.

Miss Nancy flipped open a big leather spiral book. "Yes, I still keep a paper calendar," she said, running her finger down a list of times and names. "But some-day the power will go out, and I'll be the only one who can still keep this place running and organized."

"That's very smart," my mother said. "I also keep a paper calendar as a backup in case something happens to my phone."

Miss Nancy pointed to her head and smiled. "Great minds think alike, Mrs. Dunne."

I was glad that Mom and Miss Nancy were bonding over being old-fashioned, but I really wanted to get this over with.

"Oh yes, here you are. You're next. You can have a seat until he's ready to—" she began, but then the door to Pickford's office opened and a red-faced sixth grader came out with both her parents. I wanted to reach out and grab her hand, say sorry, apologize for being a bad influence.

"Actually, you can go in right now," Miss Nancy finished.

I gulped. It was my turn.

Mom poked her head in the office and did that knocking-on-an-open door thing, which I'd always thought was weird. I mean, the door was open. Why knock on it?

Principal Pickford waved us in.

I settled myself into a chair, and Mom sat beside me. My eyes immediately went to my favorite picture on the wall, the lone palm tree on the beach. It was strangely calming. Maybe that was why the principal had kept it up there all these years.

Principal Pickford finished typing something on his computer, and then he gave us his full attention. If it was possible, he looked even more tired than usual.

"So, Mrs. Dunne, you're aware of why you're here today?"

"Very much so," Mom said.

She leaned down to pull a manila folder out of her bag and placed it on her lap. I had no idea what she'd brought, which was strange because we'd spent a long time talking the night before about my blog post. Mom was really impressed with my writing "and my ideas," she'd said. But what she had in that folder was a mystery.

"I know you're very active in our school community," Principal Pickford began.

Mom nodded. "I never miss a school committee meeting. I believe that community involvement is important, as is having a say and a seat at the table."

"Then you were there the night the committee decided to start enforcing some rules we'd unfortunately overlooked in the handbook."

"Oh, I was there. I heard Mrs. Scruggs and a few others stand up and complain."

"So you understand why the committee was motivated to make the decision that it did."

"The squeaky wheel does get the grease," Mom said.

I had no idea what that meant, but this conversation wasn't going as I had expected, and that seemed good, maybe.

Before Mr. Pickford could say anything else, Mom asked, "Were any students allowed to speak at the meeting?"

Mr. Pickford frowned, and a zillion lines formed on his forehead. "No students were at the meeting. You were there, Mrs. Dunne. You know that."

"I wonder if they would have gone to the meeting if they'd known decisions were about to be made that would affect their lives so greatly."

I watched my mother speak, clearly and calmly, legs crossed at the ankle, hands clasped over the folder on her lap, a perfect lady. But there was a fire inside her, one that I could only see in her eyes. And for the first time, I thought she kind of looked like me.

"Perhaps they would have," Principal Pickford said, waving his hand like he could wave her question away. "But the meeting already occurred."

Mom's head snapped toward mine. "How did the school committee's decision make you feel?"

"Me?" I blurted, even though, like, *duh*, she was looking at me. "Um, it made me feel lots of ways."

Mom turned back to the principal. "Could my daughter express these feelings to you right now?"

Caught off guard, Principal Pickford blinked slowly. I was sure this was the last thing on earth that he wanted to sit and listen to. He had a long line of other families waiting to come in to hear about the evils of leggings that their insolent daughters and sons had worn to school Friday. But the way my mom had worded it gave him no choice, unless he wanted to be a huge jerk. And I knew he wasn't a jerk.

"Of course," he said.

Mom motioned to me. "Go on, Riley."

I licked my lips nervously. I knew all the ways these decisions had made me feel. That was the basis of my article. But it was much easier for me to write them down than to say them out loud to my principal. A rush came over me, a tingling from my head to my toes. The way my mom had worded this . . . she'd set me up. She'd given me a chance. Mr. Pickford might never read the article I wrote. But I could recite it for him.

My chest tightened as I looked at my mother. She gave me a small smile and nodded.

It wasn't like I had my article memorized or anything, but I could remember the main points. I cleared my throat. "At first, when all these rules came at us out of nowhere, I was confused."

"There were no new rules, Riley," Principal Pickford interrupted. "They were all in the handbook."

"But they were never enforced," I said. "And all of a sudden, without warning, they were. First there were the newspaper changes."

"And how did that make you feel?" Mom prodded.

"Disappointed," I said, remembering the day. "But then that was overshadowed by all the dress-coding."

Principal Pickford cut in. "You didn't even get dress-coded that first day. Not until the day you chose to break the rules on purpose."

"But I had feelings while watching my friends get pulled out of class and sent home. Watching some of them cry. Having to sit by and see tons of girls—and only girls—miss important class time so they wouldn't be a distraction to the boys, while *certain* boys bullied and distracted us all the time." My teeth clenched as I thought about Brody taunting *Bloody Julia*.

"How did the newly enforced dress code make the other girls feel?" Mom asked, bringing me back to the subject at hand.

"Humiliated. Shamed. One girl told me that when she stood in the hallway, getting her shorts measured by a teacher, with all these kids walking by . . . she felt dirty. And my friend Stella got coded at the dance for wearing the same exact dress that I was wearing. But she was coded and I wasn't because, um, because . . ."

"She was discriminated against due to her body maturity?" Mom suggested.

"Yes. That."

"And the boys? Do you know how it made them feel?" Mom smirked as she said this. She remembered that part in my article.

"One boy confessed to me that he felt insulted. He felt that the policy assumed boys were weak-minded and easily distracted."

"That's an interesting perspective, don't you think?" Mom directed the question to Mr. Pickford, who'd stopped interrupting and was now only listening. He gave a slow nod in response.

"Also," Mom added, "it might give some of the less well-behaved boys perceived permission to taunt and disrespect girls for their bodies. If the administration was shaming the girls, why couldn't they?"

Pickford's mouth opened and closed like he was a fish out of water.

Mom turned back to me. "How did this newly enforced dress code affect your education?"

"It added some stress," I said. "Girls were worried and scared all the time about getting coded. I saw them measuring straps in the hallway and showing up late to class. Shopping for khakis the night before a test rather than studying. The whole thing was super distracting."

Mom tapped on her chin, pretending to be deep in thought. "Distracting, eh? The dress code was supposedly in place to *prevent* distractions."

Mom didn't even have to prod me this time. "It only added more distractions for the girls. And how that made me feel was that my class time and my education weren't as important as a boy's. And that if I wore leggings at school to be comfortable and a boy thought, said, or did nasty things, that it would be my fault. The boy doesn't have to stop; he doesn't have to learn to be a gentleman. The blame is on me."

Principal Pickford's face turned pale.

"And then your club was taken away," Mom said quietly.

A lump formed in my throat. Talking about this would be the hardest of all. "I loved the Red Club. Lots of girls did. We supported each other, helped each other. And when it was shut down, I felt . . . I felt . . ." I stopped and took a deep breath so that the tears wouldn't come. "I felt like the school was taking away everything I cared about. The newspaper, our comfy clothes, our support group. Walking into school every morning used to feel great. Now it felt . . . hostile."

"Hostile," my mother repeated.

She opened the folder on her lap and read out loud from a paper. "'Hawking Middle School is committed to providing an educational experience in a safe, supportive environment that fosters respect for all equally.'"

Then she closed the folder. "Do you recognize that, Mr. Pickford?"

"Of course," he said, but his voice sounded different. "That's our school's Core Values Statement."

"And you've just heard my daughter speak about how some of the recent decisions have made students feel. Disappointed, humiliated, shamed, dirty, insulted, stressed, worried, and scared. And the environment felt hostile. Does that sound like it's in accordance with our Core Values Statement?"

Mr. Pickford dragged his hands down his face and sighed. "I think you know the answer to that."

Mom closed the folder and reclasped her hands on top of it. "Then I think you know things can't stay the way they currently are. We need to make a change."

But what? Mr. Pickford couldn't overrule the school committee. There were no take-backs.

I thought about why my mom always went to those boring school committee meetings anyway. She'd told me that we couldn't complain about rules a committee made if we weren't involving ourselves when they were made. But how could I have involved myself if I wasn't on the committee?

I remembered what my mom said about having a seat at the table. An idea popped into my brain like a zap of lightning.

"We want a seat at the table!" I blurted.

Mr. Pickford's eyebrows rose. "Excuse me?"

"The handbook was created without any student input. The school committee runs without any students on it."

"I appreciate the idea," Mr. Pickford began. "But we can't add a child to the school committee. There are town bylaws and elections—"

"What about an advisor?" Mom interrupted him.

I leaned forward in my chair. "Yes! A student

advisor who attends meetings and helps to give the perspective of the students on proposed decisions." The words flowed from my mouth so naturally I was almost shocked.

Mr. Pickford looked from me to my mother and back again. "That's a bright young lady you have there."

Mom gave him a nod. "Thank you."

"And I think you have a great idea, Riley," he said, looking right at me. My chest swelled with pride. "But," he added, "I'll have to run it by the school committee members first."

My shoulders sagged. That could take days. Weeks, even!

"I'll try to reach them all via e-mail today," he added.

"Really?" I said, my voice going unnaturally high.

"Really," he said with a smile. The first smile I'd seen from him in a while.

Mom and I left the office. Thankfully, there was no one in the waiting area, because we jumped up and down and gave each other high fives. That would have looked totally weird to anyone watching.

"We worked so well together!" I said. "The way you set me up like that with your questions."

"And the way you answered them. I'm so proud of you," Mom beamed. "You were amazing in there— well-spoken, professional, and calm."

We were an awesome team. I never would have predicted it. I took her hands in mine. "Do you remember when you said you're nothing like me? That was wrong."

"What do you mean?" she asked in a quiet voice.

"I've always been proud of my way with words. Dad says it's my superskill. But what I just saw in that meeting? Wow! I knew you had a talent for negotiation. That's why you're so good at your job. But I never realized until now that *you're* who I got my superskill from." I grinned. "We're more alike than we thought."

She smiled so wide I thought she would split her face. And then she turned away, blinking fast and wiping something from her eye.

Mom left for work, and I waited around the office for Miss Nancy to return from her bathroom break or wherever she was. I needed a pass since I'd be entering my first class late.

I lowered myself onto a chair and tapped my fingers on Miss Nancy's desk. Her calendar lay open, and a thought occurred to me. I remembered what my mom had told me. *For every parent who stands up* and complains during a public meeting, there are ten more who book time with the principal to complain privately.

No, don't do it, I silently said to myself. *You literally just left the principal's office. You can't get back in trouble already.*

But the investigative-journalist side of my brain said, *It could be right there. All the answers. Just a quick peek. You wouldn't be harming anyone. . . .*

Before my rational brain could argue back, I turned the calendar around to face me and flipped back in time. My eyes scanned the names and dates, looking for anything unusual in the days before the Red Club shut down.

And then a cold feeling dropped over me. Why was *that* name there? Why would she have had an appointment with the principal? My brain slowly, reluctantly, put the pieces together. It felt like my heart had stopped.

I knew who'd complained about the Red Club.

And it was worse than I could have imagined.

CHAPTER 27

I STRUGGLED TO CONCENTRATE IN MY morning classes. I couldn't believe what I'd seen in Miss Nancy's calendar. I needed to hear the truth, right now.

As soon as the bell rang, I rushed past Ava to get to the cafeteria first and took my usual seat. I didn't bother to buy lunch. My stomach was rolling around like a clothes dryer; I wouldn't be able to eat. I just needed a minute to get my thoughts together while Ava went through the line.

Ava knew something was wrong as soon as she saw

my face. I was sure I looked like one of those cartoon characters where smoke came out of their ears.

"What's up?" she asked gingerly, laying her tray down on the table.

I gripped the edge of the table tightly. "Nothing much. Just found out that my best friend is the one who destroyed my club."

Her mouth dropped open, and her eyes immediately watered. Nothing she could say, no lies she could conjure up, could make up for what I saw on her face—the truth. It was her. When I'd seen Mrs. Clement's name written in Miss Nancy's calendar, I hadn't wanted to believe it. But it couldn't be a coincidence that Ava's mom had met with the principal the day before my club was taken away.

"Why?" I asked simply.

Ava squirmed in her seat, clearly uncomfortable, but I didn't take any delight in it. My heart was broken. Even though we weren't really speaking after our fight, we'd still supposedly been best friends when she'd gone behind my back.

"H-how did you find out?" she stammered.

"That doesn't matter," I said. "I just want to hear it from you. Why?"

Ava took a deep breath and looked away from me.

"Wednesday afternoons are my only time off. And that's when the Red Club met."

I cut in. "So because your schedule is too crazy, and I was at my club during the one hour you had free every week, you had to take it away from me?"

"No!" she cried, and a couple of heads turned. "It wasn't like that. I'm not explaining it well."

I crossed my arms over my chest. "I don't know how you *could* explain this. It makes no sense. You knew how much I loved that club."

"Yes, I did! And I would have loved it too, if I'd been allowed in."

I leaned forward, my voice rising. "What do you mean, allowed? You would have been in the club when—"

She interrupted. "Just because I wasn't bleeding yet, that didn't mean I had no questions. I need support too. I need friends. I need . . . time away from gymnastics. But I wasn't allowed in your little club." When she spat out the words, I saw more than anger and bitterness. I saw that she'd been really hurt.

"You could have asked to—" I began.

"I did!" she yelled. Everyone at our table was listening now. "Anytime I tried to talk to you about the Red Club, you just pushed it off and told me I'd get my period soon. But I didn't want my period. I wanted friendship. I wanted to hang out with you and maybe even the other girls too."

I sat back in my chair, hard. At least, in a twisted way, it made sense now. She'd killed my club because she was lonely. She was so busy with gymnastics, and the only open time was when I was having fun with my other friends. A group I wouldn't let her join.

"It was a selfish thing to do," she said, tears streaming down her face now. Half the cafeteria seemed to be staring at us. "But I thought that if I couldn't join the club, then maybe it shouldn't exist. If the club was gone, I'd be able to hang out with you again on my afternoon off. So I convinced my mother that the reason I'd been so upset lately was because of this club that wouldn't let me join because I didn't have my period. And she complained to the principal that a club like that shouldn't exist in school."

My chest heaved up and down with deep breaths. So many emotions flickered through me that I could barely keep track. But despite how angry I was, I still had to know. "What was the real reason you'd been upset?"

She threw her hands up in the air. "There are too many to name. I'm tired all the time. The girls at my gym don't like me. I feel like everyone at school belongs and I don't. I miss *you*." She shook her head. "And what I did solved none of that. I'm still tired. The girls at the gym are the same. And now you hate me."

"I don't hate you," I muttered.

She inhaled quickly, hope lighting up her face.

"But I'm not ready to forgive you. And I don't know if I ever will be."

I stood up, my metal chair screeching against the cafeteria floor. Then I ran to the bathroom, where I thought I might hide forever.

The bathroom door opened, and many footsteps shuffled in.

Camille's face peeked under the stall door. "She's in this one!" She pounded her fist on the door. "C'mon, Riley, open up."

I slid the lock and let the door swing open. Camille, Stella, and Cee were clustered together with concerned looks on their faces.

"How did you know I wasn't actually using the toilet?" I asked.

Cee tossed her braids over her shoulder. "Because you've been in here forever and everyone told us what went down at lunch."

The story was probably all over school by now. I felt a pinch of pity for Ava and pushed it away.

"Was Ava really the one who complained about the Red Club?" Stella asked.

I nodded, though I could still barely believe it. "What are you guys doing in here?" I asked. "You're going to miss lunch."

It was then that I noticed Cee and Camille holding paper lunch bags.

"We decided to come find you," Cee said. And then she and Camille sat on an old broken radiator by the wall and started to eat their sandwiches.

Stella gave them a disgusted look. "I was going to buy lunch today, but I'm all set without eating in an E. coli closet. I'll eat when I get home." She glanced at me. "Making sure you're okay is more important."

"If it makes you feel any better," Cee said through a bite, "your blog post has taken off. Everyone in school is reading it. They're even sharing it with their friends in other towns."

"Cool," I said, and I meant it. That did make me feel a little bit better. And today hadn't been all bad. The meeting with Principal Pickford had actually gone really well.

"So, fill us in," Camille said.

And I did. From my spot in the bathroom stall, I told them all about what Ava had done and why. And I shared my hope that Principal Pickford would convince the school committee to allow a student advisor. We needed any glimmer of hope right now.

CHAPTER 28

THE REST OF THE SCHOOL DAY WAS A blur. I missed half of history class due to hiding in the bathroom, but the gossip must have reached the teachers' lounge, because Mr. Spaulding just gave me a sympathetic look and didn't even ask for a late pass. By the end of the day the light buzz that had been building in my brain had turned into a headache. I couldn't wait to get home and throw myself on the couch. But after the last bell, when I was on my way to my locker, Principal Pickford came over the intercom, once again summoning me to his office.

"Oooohhh," a few kids teased in that *you're in trouble* tone as I passed by. It was good to know that even as many things changed, some stayed the same.

Miss Nancy was on the phone at her desk as I walked in. She waved me toward Mr. Pickford's office and mouthed, *Go right in.*

I settled into what I mentally referred to now as "my usual seat" and stared at the photo of the palm tree on the wall. But I didn't have long to zone out because Mr. Pickford came in quickly and sat across from me.

"I heard back from the school committee members," he began.

Wow, that was quick, I thought. *Too quick? They said no. They definitely said no.*

"They agreed."

"What?" I said, stunned.

"The student-advisor position is a go. They don't want it to be voted on by the students, though, because sometimes those become popularity contests."

I nodded. I still remembered last year, when all the jocks voted for Brody for class president and he did nothing all year. Literally nothing.

"How will the advisor be chosen?" I asked.

"The principal will choose. So for right now, that

means me. And I choose you. If you'll accept."

Now my world was really rocked. Like, it was a good thing I was in my usual seat and not standing.

"Um, thank you. Definitely, I accept."

"Don't thank me yet. This role will have a lot of work involved. Especially since I also convinced the school committee to update the handbook. It hasn't been done in years, and while I agree that whatever rules are written in the handbook should be enforced, perhaps it's time to update some of them. You will be involved in that process and sit in on those meetings."

My pulse raced. We could change the dress code. We could change so many things. . . . My mind started spinning with the possibilities, but then I realized Mr. Pickford was still talking.

"And I would like to bring Ms. Bhatt back to her role as advisor at the newspaper, but I will still require story approval before anything is posted online."

"Isn't that censorship?" I asked.

He let out a heavy sigh. "We could have gotten sued for that chicken-nugget article, Riley."

"You wouldn't have gotten sued for the article. You would have gotten sued for the mistake in the cafeteria. I only shined a light on it."

"You should have come to me first."

"But if I did that, you would have shut the story down. And it was important that people knew the mistake happened."

Principal Pickford took a deep breath. "But if we'd worked together, the story could have had a comment from me detailing what we're doing to make sure the supplier's mistake never happens again. And that would have prevented the several calls I received from very worried parents that day."

Oh. That did make sense. I just assumed Mr. Pickford would have killed the story completely. But maybe he wouldn't have, if I had given him the chance.

"So Ms. Bhatt will return?"

"Yes, with our new approval rule in place."

It was a compromise, but one that could work out. Since he was in such a negotiating mood, I asked, "What about the Red Club? If we got an advisor, could we have meetings again?"

He grimaced. "I don't know, Riley. You girls have health classes and the Internet. Information is everywhere."

"It's not just information. It's support. It's—"

He put up a hand. "I know, I know. If I've learned anything in the last week, it's how much that club meant to you girls. But we do get complaints. Some parents may not want their daughters to receive information from the Red Club."

I shrugged. "Simple. Then their daughters don't go. Some parents don't want their kids to play football because of concussions, but you don't get rid of the whole team."

His mouth twitched, like he was holding back a smile. "If this reporter thing doesn't pan out, I think you'd have a bright career as a lawyer."

"Does that mean the Red Club can come back?"

I watched his glasses slowly slip down his nose as he thought for a long moment. Then he pushed them back up. "The Red Club can come back if you have an advisor and if all members bring in permission slips signed from their parents."

"Done!" I slapped the top of his desk, maybe a little too enthusiastically, but he just laughed. "I'll have no problem finding an advisor."

"I'm sure Miss Nancy will volunteer," he said. "It's about time she made that official."

Official? Miss Nancy? She was the person behind the scenes! The one who made sure our locker was never taken. That we had the library reserved on Wednesday afternoons. That our emergency stash was always stocked. It had been Miss Nancy the whole time.

Principal Pickford was gazing up at the photo on the wall, my favorite one, of the palm tree, and a dreamy look came over his face. "This is my last semester at Hawking Middle School. I'm retiring."

I felt myself sink deeply into the chair. Despite the times we disagreed, I really liked Principal Pickford.

"I hope it's not because of all the chaos we caused this week," I said.

"Of course not," he said with a chuckle. "This has been planned for a long time. I'm retiring because I've saved enough, I'm old enough, and Florida is calling my name. I tried to retire over the summer, but the superintendent begged me to stay for a few more months while she completed her search for a replacement. I agreed, as long as I'd get out of here before the second semester and all that snow."

"Oh, well, congratulations, then." I started to get up from my chair, but he motioned for me to sit back down.

"Do you know who my favorite student is?" he asked.

I held back a sigh. Not this conversation again. I repeated his own words back at him. "Your favorite students are the ones you don't see. The ones who never cause you trouble."

"Actually, I've changed my mind about that. My favorite students are the ones who make me think. You, Riley Dunne, are my favorite student."

If my jaw could have unhinged itself and fallen to the floor, it would have. "What?"

"I wanted to sail through these last couple of months with as little drama as possible. And maybe that's part of why I gave in to certain parents rather than consider the broader implications. Your mom was spot-on with her squeaky-wheel comment." He looked at me meaningfully. "But I'm glad this happened. You challenged me, Riley. Facing a challenge isn't always easy or fun, but you learn from it. You're going to change the world, Riley Dunne. And I'll be watching . . . from my pool float in Florida."

And, in a rare moment, I found myself speechless.

CHAPTER 29

THE DUNNE FAMILY DINNER GAME WAS my best yet. I took so long that my turn lasted all through the meal and everyone else had to go during dessert. And later that night I got a text from Cee that my blog post's views were in the *hundreds*. People were really liking it and sharing it. This was good timing, with our club coming back. We'd have no trouble recruiting new members.

Tuesday morning, I strutted into school with my head held high for the first time in weeks. I wasn't feeling down or hopeless or angry. In fact, I couldn't stop smiling. I felt giddy.

And that only intensified when I saw who was waiting for me at my locker.

Cole pushed himself off the wall and waved as I approached. "I just heard the good news. You're getting your club back!"

"And Ms. Bhatt is returning to the newspaper! With a little compromise. But I think things are going to be great, actually."

He smiled. "I think you're great, actually."

I laughed, and he grinned shyly.

"That was cheesy, wasn't it?"

I shrugged. "Yeah, but I liked it."

"And I like you."

"Okay, now *that* was cheesy." I grinned, and added, "But I like you too."

His face turned the brightest red I'd ever seen. Worse than the time Danny got a sunburn at the beach.

"Cool," he said. "Can I text you later?"

"Sure!"

And then he and his cute red face ran off.

I put a hand on my chest as my breathing slowly started to return to normal. I'd done it. I'd really done it! It was only a couple of weeks ago that I'd been scared to even make small talk with Cole at newspaper meetings, and now I'd told him I *liked* him. I'd never felt this brave. I felt like I could do anything!

The school day was awesome. I paid attention better in my classes because I wasn't worried about everything else—other than avoiding Ava in math and at lunch. But that was pretty easy because she was avoiding me too. And once the announcement was made about my advisor job, so many people—boys and girls—had ideas for updates to the handbook. They were excited that they'd actually be represented this time, by one of their own.

After the last bell, I was about to head to my locker when Stella and Camille each grabbed one of my arms and pulled me into the library, where Cee was waiting, staring at something on her phone.

"What?" I said, pulling my arms back. "What is it?"

"It's your blog post." Cee looked up at me, and her eyes were rimmed with red. She reached out, handing me her phone.

I steeled myself for the worst. What now? Just when things were starting to look up. Had someone gotten my post removed somehow? Was I in trouble again?

But as I glanced down at the phone in my hand, I saw that the post was still there.

"Scroll down to the comments," Cee said, her voice tight, like she was trying not to cry.

I scrolled with my finger, stopping when I reached the bottom of the article. My finger froze. *Two hundred fifty-seven comments.* When we'd hit a hundred views, we'd only had five comments. How was this number possible?

I glanced up, hoping for some sort of explanation.

"Sometime today you went viral," Cee explained. "Everyone's been sharing it far and wide, and it crossed the Twitter feed of some big-time reporter. She reposted it to all her followers. And then thousands of other people retweeted. And it just blew up from there. I can't even keep up!"

My mouth opened as I turned her words around in my head. All those people had read my article? And they'd liked it enough to share when they didn't even know me?

Stella leaned over my shoulder. "Just start reading."

The first comment was only one word. *Cool.*

Others came quickly after that.

This is a great idea.

I wish we had a Red Club at my school.

What an empowering idea for young women. I would fully support this at the school where I teach.

I'm going to try to start a Red Club at my middle school!

It continued, on and on, comment after comment.

"You started something," Cee said. "Really started something. It's going to be bigger than us. Bigger than our school."

And then I understood why her eyes had been all glassy and red, because mine had started to water too. A single tear first, then another, streaming down my cheeks. I couldn't control it.

I took the bus home in a state of shock. We made plans to meet at my house and talk about how to make the Red Club even bigger. I had some ideas of my own and shared them in our group text. I was so lost in thought I nearly missed my stop.

But then I noticed Ava get up and walk down the aisle.

Ava . . . why was she on the bus? She always got picked up from school because her mom had to rush her to the gym.

It was weird, following her down the sidewalk to our houses, neither of us speaking, not even acknowledging the other's presence. I hated it. What she'd done was terrible and selfish, but I kind of understood it. I hadn't handled things perfectly either. But I had a plan to make sure no one felt left out like that ever again.

Ava stopped as the sidewalk met her driveway; then she slowly turned around to face me.

"I heard you got your club back." She was always tiny, but she looked even smaller now, her shoulders hunched, her face staring at the ground.

"Yeah, I did," I said flatly.

"I'm really glad," she said. "I read your blog post. It was amazing." Her voice began to tremble. "I'm so sorry, Riley."

"I know you are," I said quickly. I didn't want her to cry again.

"I talked to my mom last night and told her the whole thing was wrong. I never should have asked her to complain to the principal. I even thought I could have her call again and say she'd changed her mind."

"We don't need that now, but thanks."

"My mom and I had a good talk," she said. "A long one. I'm cutting back on gymnastics."

I reared back, surprised. "Really?"

"Yeah, I'm going to have three afternoons a week off now. My mom said I'll probably fall behind the other girls, but . . ." She shrugged as her voice trailed off.

I knew that had been a tough decision for her. She loved gymnastics, and she was so good at it. But it had clearly been too much lately. I didn't quite know what to say, so I settled on "I hope it makes you feel better."

Ava nodded, scraping her sneaker back and forth against the ground. "Could I . . . um . . . could I still join the Red Club?"

I watched her for a minute. She'd betrayed me. But part of the reason was because I'd shut her out.

"I've had a lot of time to think about things, and I wanted to say sorry too," I said.

"What for?" she asked.

"For not letting you in the club to begin with. Traditions don't have to stay the same. I should have pushed to let kids who didn't have their period yet join if they wanted to. Especially when one was my best friend. We're changing the club rules so no one else will feel left out like you did. It wasn't fair, and I'm sorry."

Her face crumpled up like she was fighting back tears, but happy ones this time.

"It's still going to meet on Wednesdays," I said. "I hope you'll have time with your different schedule."

"I'll make time!" she said enthusiastically. "It's important. *You're* important . . . to me."

I saw a flash of something—the old Ava, the old us.

I aimed a thumb at my front door. "Cee and the girls are coming over for some Red Club planning. My mom bought ice cream. Do you want to come over too?"

"Yeah!" she said, with a smile so bright it could charge up a lightbulb. "I really do."

Cee brought her laptop, and we spent the afternoon at my dining room table creating an official Red Club website. It was a little awkward with Ava at first, but the girls followed my lead. Forgiveness felt good. Not ice cream good, but hardly anything feels ice cream good.

We changed some of the rules of the club, to make it more inclusive. And we uploaded instructions on how other girls could create Red Clubs in their schools, with suggestions on meetings and tips from everything we'd learned.

By the end of the week the Red Club had forty-three chapters in the United States and fifteen more across the globe.

We never truly know how our actions will affect people. I didn't know our little movement would lead to the largest number of students sent home in the same day in Hawking Middle School history. I didn't know my blog post would spread so far, so quickly.

We'd wanted to create change in our school, and we ended up inspiring girls all over the world.

And *that* felt ice cream good.

Acknowledgments

Hugs and thanks to these awesome people:

My agent, Kate Schafer Testerman, who loved this idea from day one.

My editor, Alyson Heller, who helped me shape the book with enthusiasm and insight.

The rest of the team at Aladdin/Simon & Schuster for their support and hard work, including Mara Anastas, Fiona Simpson, Chriscynethia Floyd, Rebecca Vitkus, and Tiara Iandiorio (for designing the cover of my dreams).

My friends who, when I announced that I was writing a period book, said, "Of course you are."

You, yes you, for reading this book, telling your friends, and spending your time with my Riley.

And finally, endless thanks to my family—Mom and Dad, the in-laws, Mike, and Ryan. I couldn't do any of this without your support and cheerleading. I love you!

Looking for another great book?
Find it
IN THE MIDDLE.

Fun, fantastic books for kids
in the in-be**TWEEN** age.

IntheMiddleBooks.com

SIMON & SCHUSTER
Children's Publishing   /SimonKids   @SimonKids

Mount Laurel Library
100 Walt Whitman Avenue
Mount Laurel, NJ 08054-9539
856-234-7319
www.mountiaurellibrary.org